STEALING LOVE

A HEART OF THE SEA ADVENTURE

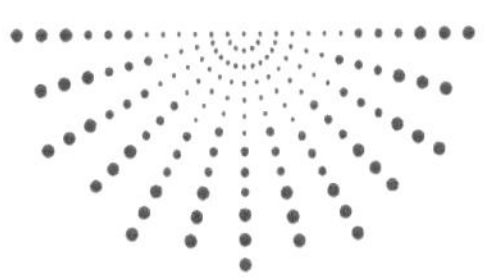

CORRINA LAWSON

SUMMER DEVON

CONTENTS

CHAPTER ONE

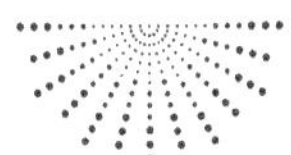

Rob wanted to gawk. He decided the persona he'd adopted for this job would do just that and let himself stare around, up, and down.

The *Heart of the Ocean*, the cruise ship that would be the scene of his latest job, rose high over the dock, more massive than he'd expected. Yes, he'd gone over the specs and blueprints. But seeing it in three dimensions gave him new appreciation for its size.

Still, all to the good. The bigger the ship, the more people on it, the easier to blend in, the easier to get the job done. Rob strolled past the enthusiastic greeters at the top of the walkway to the ship, found a steward to deliver his luggage to his cabin, and headed straight for the art gallery.

The map he'd memorized of the ship served him well.

The only problem was that the gallery was nearly empty, which meant Rob attracted attention from the clerk on duty. Just his luck that the clerk would zoom in on him, preventing a quiet stroll around the spacious wood-paneled room that was the showcase of a collection of artifacts from the *Siren*, a famous shipwreck, and jewelry inspired by that shipwreck.

First, the clerk tried to engage Rob with a tray of ugly pinky rings.

Next, and more interesting, the clerk brought his attention to an exquisite jade-and-bone carving, marked up about fifteen times its actual worth.

Rob shrugged apologetically. "Sorry, Just window-shopping. It's really pretty, but no."

The clerk frowned, perhaps contemplating whether to continue this hard sell. Begone, Rob thought. Nothing he was wearing indicated an ability to afford any of this. Rob had dressed in standard drab middle-class gear. He'd even taken off his Rolex Submariner. Maybe the gallery guy was just trying to stay in practice.

Rob must have made his disinterest clear at last, because the clerk stopped bugging him and stared down at his own polished fingernails instead.

Rob had hoped that soon after departure would be his best chance for a discreet look, but he'd underestimated the need of the other passengers to get settled. There was only one other passenger window-shopping, a blonde with a pink hairband, who had walked in about five minutes after he had. She now lingered too close to the center display that held the most luxurious items on board, worth millions of dollars, her eyes wide in appreciation.

Even the clerk knew she wasn't a serious shopper, and he'd retreated to the other side of the gallery.

Rob craved to discreetly spec out his true target. But no, the little blonde kept walking around the center case, gawking at the diamond necklace as if it held the answer to her dreams. Since he couldn't study the case with her in the way, Rob drifted closer and watched her instead.

Her denim skirt and cheap floral blouse almost swamped her small body. No way on earth or sea could a woman like her afford the goods for sale in this gallery, especially not *that* necklace and earrings.

She faced away from him, her hands clasped at her back as if stopping herself from reaching for the treasure. Her long shiny hair lacked any sort of styling. Her hands at the small of her back had nails cut short and unpolished. He played a guessing game with himself: elementary school teacher or dental hygienist? Enough curiosity niggled at him that he considered falling into conversation with her, but he had no desire to be noticed on this journey.

She leaned over the display and fiddled with her own unremarkable enamel earring, black with a white floral design. She stared hungrily at the diamond pendants that went with the necklace.

Rob wanted to chase away her wistful expression, maybe by telling her that her delicate all-American features would match better with finer, less clunky jewelry than those ostentatious million-dollar pieces.

But that would be a lie, because the blonde had the sort of face and features that would look equally good with either flashy diamonds or a simple slender gold chain.

He knew about stones and precious metals, but he was hardly an expert in which designs went with which sort of face. He trusted facts and figures. They were reliable. People were not. They had all sorts of ridiculous wants and needs.

And Bob the surety bond attorney, his role for the length of the cruise, would be even more awkward than Rob the corporate thief around women.

The blonde must have felt Rob's stare because she straightened, turned, and looked directly into his face. Her eyes widened, just a little, as if he seemed as yummy as the diamonds. Someone else wouldn't notice that regard, but Rob had trained himself to pay attention to details.

And then she smiled at him.

Instant irrational attraction struck him, like a blow right in the solar plexus. His mouth went dry, his heart beat faster, and it wasn't with fear for a change. He could ignore fear. He had no intention of paying attention to *this* response either.

Rob liked women, all kinds of women. Tall, short, well-dressed, in hiking boots, in nothing at all, so long as they liked him back, but this sort of wide-eyed cute...*girl* was off-limits. No, wait. She was a woman: full-grown and, judging from the creases at the corners of her eyes as she smiled, at least twenty-five. Still, he couldn't try to charm an innocent from the Midwest or wherever, even if it would make their cruise more interesting. Besides, she already clearly desired what she couldn't have. She'd likely be trouble, more trouble than he could afford on this trip.

But he stared at the smile and those beautifully even white teeth—did she have veneers? Probably not since they weren't quite perfect. The indentation at the corner of her mouth, nearly a dimple, was absolutely perfect.

Damn. Was gawking at a woman's teeth part of his persona? She'd only turned to face him moments before, but too much time had passed to pretend there hadn't been some sort of silent interaction between them. He had to say something.

"Real nice gems, aren't they?" he asked her, letting his awkward self out. "I never saw anything like it. Is that some kinda nautical design? Oh yes, indeed, look at that. Pretty!"

"So pretty," she agreed. "Didn't even know they'd travel with something so pricey on board. Did you?"

"Not so much, but I guess they need something to show off to the passengers who have suites." He didn't want to appear too interested, but he put out his hand for her to shake. Bob would do that, right? Bob was a polite person. "I'm Bob. This your first cruise? It's mine."

He probably laid the "aw shucks" on a bit hard.

She had small hands but a strong, warm grip. "Hey, hello, Bob. I'm May. My first cruise too! It's so exciting to be on board, isn't it?" She let go of him and waved her hand at the display, still wearing that bright smile. "I'm just looking, of course. I expect if I looked like a real customer, that elegant man would be out here offering to help me."

Sense of humor and self-deprecating too. He'd find out her full name and then head online to discover what he could about her, because…

He wanted to.

Don't be memorable, he reminded himself. Not to anyone. Friendly and nothing more.

But then the words came out before he could stop them. "Want to go for a walk outside? We might see the last of the port."

She glanced back at the display. "Sure," she said.

Outside on deck, the air was already cooler and softer with salt. She leaned over and gazed at the seagulls following them. The sound of the water crashing against the ship and the growl of the engines was almost drowned out by the excited chatter of the crowd, all goggle-eyed at leaving on their cruise.

Rob envied them that innocent eagerness—joy that May evidently shared.

"It's so amazing," she said softly, gripping the railing tightly. "I can tell the ocean is so vast already, and we're barely underway." She tilted her head back. "We have nothing like this back home. Ha. But that's just what you said, isn't it? I guess nearly everyone on board says that at least once per trip. I'm glad to get that cliché out of the way."

Enchanting. "What do you do back home, wherever that is?"

"I teach kindergarten. I've been saving up for this trip forever. I can hardly believe it's my chance now." Her forehead wrinkled. "And you, Bob?"

"I review surety bond contracts."

"Oh."

He paused. "Did you just wince at me?"

She gave a snort of laughter, then went a little pink. "I guess I did, because I'm supposed to follow up with something like 'Wow, that sounds interesting,' and I have to tell you, it really doesn't. I'm not even sure what surety bonds are."

He laughed too. "Yeah, well, get a couple of beers in me and I can't help telling you all about how to underwrite a bond so as to make the insurance company's liability limited."

"Who buys surety bonds?" she asked.

"Companies. Construction companies. Mine owners." He looked around. "Cruise ship companies."

"Oh! Did your company do that for this one?"

He chuckled. "No, we mostly bond construction companies. I wouldn't know how to evaluate a cruise ship. I guess maybe making sure the engines are certified and they have proper drinking water since we'll be in the middle of the ocean?"

That all sounded right, he hoped. He'd quizzed his friend the surety lawyer a few times to become Bob. What he'd learned: keep it boring. And that wasn't hard with surety bonds.

She frowned. "So you're saying there might be a problem with the drinking water on board?"

"Maybe?" Wow, that was a logic leap. "I mean, as an attorney, I'd want to know about the process before I bonded it."

"I am curious about how they recycle the drinking water on a ship." Her eyes crinkled again. "I help out the older students with the science fair. One of them this year had something about water filtration. They must do it on a grand scale on this ship, and so…"

She halted midsentence. "Bob, did I say something wrong?"

Gah, his mind must have wandered. "No, but I thought you weren't interested in surety bonds," he said drily.

"Oh." She stared at the deck, deflated. "Sorry. I guess I'm bad at this small-talk thing. Too much talking to kids, I guess."

He'd made this ray of sunshine sad. That was no good. "Hey, I guess I'm bad at this too. Let me make it up to you." He offered his arm. "Let's try strolling along the deck, see if we're good at that?"

She brightened. "Deal!"

They walked along the deck, her arm hooked in his. No skin touching, of course. He had on a long-sleeved shirt, and she wore a windbreaker. But still, it felt intimate in a way being close to someone hadn't felt like in a long time.

He really should stay away from her.

He used the walk to examine other passengers and the crew, but he did have to pay attention to her too because she seemed to notice everything, pointing out parts of the ship, like the bridge, the pool deck above them, guessing at which kids belonged to which parents, and wistfully staring at the klatch of women traveling together.

Kindergarten teachers, right? So used to watching at least a dozen kids at a time that she automatically sized up an environment. No wonder she paid such close attention to her first time on a ship.

They had to unlock arms as someone brushed between them, almost knocking her into the rail.

"Hey!" Bob yelled after the guy, but was ignored. "You okay?" he said to her.

"It's okay," she said. "Kids don't always look where they're going either."

"Yeah, but they're usually not taller than you."

She giggled—somehow cute on her—and they started off in the same direction, but not touching anymore. He missed having her closer.

Her innocent form of flirtation was fun, perhaps because she was having fun too. Spray rose up from the ocean, and she reached out, grabbed his arm, and pointed at the water. "Oh look! A school of something. Whales? Dolphins?"

He peered at the seemingly tiny figures in the ocean kicking up white foam. "I have no idea, but we could find someone who knows. An expert."

"But then we'd lose sight of them. I want to watch!"

And she did, with wide-eyed abandon again. In a few minutes, the dolphins—if that was what they were—seemed to vanish, and then she stared at her hand on his button-down business shirt. She smiled as she gave a tentative squeeze of his biceps.

"You sure have a lot of muscles for a surety bond insurance person."

"We do have gyms back home. Maybe not as high-tech as the ones here on this ship, but..."

"Yes, of course you would. Sorry!" She removed her hand quickly, as if only just realizing what she'd done. "Let me try this adult-conversation thing again. Where are you from?"

He was going to say Texas, but she might be from there herself, so he picked the area he'd most recently visited. "Near Baltimore," he said. He pointed out to sea. "Aw, there're the dolphins are again, but they're headed away. I expect they don't like the big engines on the boat. Now, if we could get a smaller motorboat or even a sailboat, that would make for a good time looking at the sea life."

"When we get to our first port of call, right? Oh, I'd love that. Is that something the company offers? I haven't looked at the list of onshore activities. I was so busy about the logistics of getting on board. I've never been to Miami before either, and it was so bright and colorful yesterday that I wandered around instead of doing my cruise planning."

"You do like the colorful. Like the jewelry in the gallery," he teased.

Her eyes widened again. Just for a moment.

And then she laughed. "A girl can dream, right?"

But had that been alarm in her blue eyes? His interest shifted to suspicion. Can't trust people, he reminded himself. They weren't logical, and he'd bet this Midwestern girl with her expressive eyes and frequent laughter ran on emotion, not logic.

They strolled to the bow, now occupied by only a few passengers, and he so enjoyed leaning against the rail, staring into the ocean and all its possibilities, his fingers lightly touching her forearm, that he nearly forgot his suspicion and his job—okay, never that, but he did relax.

Maybe the tiny shifts in her face were just her idiosyncratic features. Perhaps she wore contacts that were drying out because she was staring at him—which she did often. That bright laser-sharp attention of hers both intrigued and dismayed him.

He liked her and wished he could do something to really make those eyes go wide and maybe make her cheeks pinken again. As he gazed up at the display of lights artfully draped over fake bushes near the café, he imagined pocketing the object he'd vowed to lift from the gallery and, as an afterthought, grabbing the necklace and earrings just for her.

In a few months, he'd send them to her—she probably lived in a drab town house where the jewels would sparkle like they came from another world. He'd have them delivered with no note. Would she know who'd sent them along? Not if he did his job right.

He realized he was so lost in his daydream that four people had passed him, and he'd done nothing to memorize their faces or size them up.

Hell. He wasn't here to flirt or enjoy himself. He'd come aboard for one reason only. The plain silver item in the case next to the diamonds was his target. But then she shifted closer, her fingers around his forearm, and he was lost again.

Dammit, remember. One last job. Rob was going to get that Siren's Song and win final say on the family projects. He loved his grandfather, but someday that reckless man would get them all thrown in prison. Sunny was Exhibit A in why most people were unpredictable and not to be trusted.

But he patted the fingers on his arm and wished he were on this cruise to have fun.

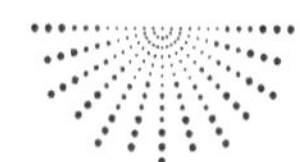

CHAPTER TWO

What was the point of being blonde if you couldn't have fun?

But, still, Miri needed to get to work. She sighed deeply, with real disappointment, as she extricated herself from Bob. It'd felt good, calming, centering, to stand at the bow with him and stare at the water. She *liked* being on this cruise ship. She liked his adorkable uncertainty. It seemed real, not fake.

"Have to go?" he asked, putting on an air of disappointment.

Bob was being polite. His attention had been wandering the last few minutes.

"I have to go figure out my schedule aboard the ship now that we're underway." She gave him May's 1000-watt smile. "See you around?"

"Sure!" And he smiled back. "I can give you my cabin number if you give me yours."

She blinked. He winced. "Oops. That came out wrong again, didn't it?"

Instead of answering, she laid her hand on his forearm, struck again by the strength he seemed to be hiding. "Tell you what, how about phone numbers? You get settled, I'll get settled, and if we still want to talk to each other…."

He almost flushed. He was seriously adorable and in all the right places.

"Deal," he said, and they exchanged numbers. If he became a problem, she could always block him.

She waved gaily as she left. Maybe he'd be good cover for May. A sweet shipboard romance. Who'd suspect one of them to be a thief?

In no time, she reached her cabin which was so boring, she wished she'd stayed with Bob.

He was well-built for an insurance guy. Bob probably spent hours working out at the company gym, hoping for some adventure in his life. That was probably why he'd taken a cruise on his own. Nice guy too, because he'd watched her face, not other parts of her anatomy, and listened to her.

She could spice up his life. Make his trip memorable.

She shook her head. Keep it innocent, otherwise he might get too close. Besides, May the kindergarten teacher wouldn't be someone who would spice up Bob's life. May was here to experience things new to her, to have the vacation of a lifetime, and she might flirt, she might have a fun time hanging out with Bob, but May wasn't the type to hop into bed with someone she just met. People like May did not steal hearts.

Miri, of course, was here to steal something else entirely.

All those lovely jewels tempted her, but no, Grandfather Jacob wanted the somewhat worthless sterling silver boatswain's pipe, nicknamed "the Siren's Song," something that only added a little color to the Siren exhibit, not something worth much money on its own. But it was worth nearly everything to her. If this job was successful, Jacob had told her that not only could she quit the family business to pursue her art, but he'd pay her what he owed her, an amount that was in the seven figures by now.

She'd agreed to the deal immediately. Only later had she wondered what the damn catch to all this was. Still no answer to that one.

Not that she hadn't researched the pipe later and discovered the legend surrounding it. Supposedly, if you blew three notes in the presence of the one you love, your love would be eternal.

Rubbish, of course. But Miri guessed her grandfather wanted it because one of his demanding clients had commissioned the thing. Another millionaire with a whim. At least Jacob had left it up to her to decide how to steal it.

She grinned as she flipped open her suitcase, removed the false bottom, and pulled out *her* silver boatswain's pipe, a dead ringer for the "Siren" pipe. She'd studied photos of the Siren pipe and spent a little bit to acquire one of the same age.

Then she'd gotten to work and made it into an exact duplicate, right down to the tiny scratches from its decades underwater and the slight discoloration from the salt of the sea. Not her usual work, she liked larger pieces, big bold colorful things of steel or marble, but this had been a fun challenge.

The best thefts, she knew, were the ones no one knew had happened.

Jacob's jobs gave her a thrill but ultimately left her empty. Some nights she lost sleep thinking about the people she'd potentially harmed. She wanted, no, *needed*, to commit to her own work. There was so much she wanted to create. This was her chance—if she did this right, Jacob would set her free.

She'd picked the kindergarten teacher persona because "May" could fade into the background and never become a suspect if anything went awry. She'd learned from experience if she went too mousy, people would notice. If she went too vixen, the same. But May was nice, friendly, and not particularly remarkable. Really, Bob was the perfect sort of guy for her.

She'd make the swap quietly, and then she'd start the rest of her life without Jacob holding money or obligation over her to control her.

A knock sounded on the cabin door. May looked through the keyhole. Grandfather Jacob. Checking up on her already? Yes, of course he was.

She opened it a crack. "Yes, sir?"

He frowned, glasses low on his nose, looking harmless, not the shark she knew he was. The man was hardly decrepit. He was sixty-five and looked twenty years younger, even with the gray he'd added to his hair. He did need the glasses, but not those oversize nerdy black ones.

"Excuse me, miss. I think I'm lost. Is this the lido deck?" he asked.

May stifled a curse. "Come in, sir. I've got a map of the layout of the ship on my phone. I'll see what I can do," she said for the benefit of anyone else in the hallway.

"I hate those smartphones. I do appreciate your help."

She gestured him in. Once she closed the door, she rounded on him. "I thought we weren't supposed to have contact on the ship, Mr. *Mazie*?"

Grandfather Jacob shrugged. "Just wanted to see if you were settled in, Miriam."

She hid a wince at her full name. She hated it. He knew that too. He liked to remind her there was nothing she could do about it.

He glanced at the room, which consisted of a closed porthole, bed, tiny desk, and equally tiny bathroom. "This is smaller than I expected."

"I suppose you have a stateroom," she said. "Concierge class? Balcony?"

He smiled. "I suppose I do."

"You're enjoying this."

He tipped the straw hat he'd somehow acquired in the hour he'd been on board. "More than I thought, yes," he confessed. "I'd forgotten how long it's been since I've taken a vacation."

Was that a crack in his reserve?

"Have you forgotten I'm not allowed to take one either?"

He shrugged. "If you handle your assignment well, you can decide on your own vacations."

Somehow, he made that sound like a threat. Yep, still the same, even with a straw hat. "You *will* stay out of my way?" she asked, though it was more of a demand.

"I will stay out of your way."

"No sabotaging me?"

"Of course not. I do keep my word, Miriam."

His only saving grace. He would badger and guilt anyone into anything. He would withhold affection—and her *money and freedom*—and give her the silent treatment. Yet once he gave his word, he kept it.

"Let's hope you don't sabotage yourself, eh?"

She put her hands on her hips. "What does that mean?"

"It means, as much as you complain about our work, you're good at it. There are no such guarantees with your art. Are you willing to take the risk that you're good enough? Are you sure you can be a success? I'd hate for you to find your new life, ah, disappointing, emotionally speaking. You don't want to feel like a fraud. I know you enjoy our work and you're definitely not a fraud at that."

He waggled a finger at her, a familiar gesture.

Anger flared, then nerves, as his question targeted her self-doubts. Maybe she was afraid. Maybe that was why she'd hadn't tried harder until now to break from him.

No, dammit, this was his fault, letting him keep her at his beck and call, knowing she'd nowhere else to turn after her mother walked away from their family, then her father decided he had to spend her childhood finding himself.

I can become a success on my own.

She said, "Look, Jacob, there are some nice-looking men aboard. That might be a distraction for you." It'd get him out of her hair and stop him from filling her head with doubts.

He shrugged. "I noticed. But many gay men who've lived to be my age seem to have brought their wives. Still playing the part."

"You make it sound like you're a rare specimen."

Jacob sighed, his only response to her attempt to make him smile. She did admire how he'd never made a secret of being gay. And, as in all things, he had rigid standards for possible relationships. The person had to be close to his own age, had to be openly gay—"*I have enough secrets already*"—and be utterly uninterested in how Jacob obtained his money. His lovers were allowed to be close, but not too close.

"No wonder you're single most of the time," she said. "You never let anyone get close enough."

"My life is my own." He glared at her. "I would remind you that I avoid civilians while on a job and expect you to do the same. I saw you walking the deck with someone already."

"Bob the surety guy? Yeah, that's not a thing. I'm all about the work. Like you, apparently. But here's a difference: I'm looking forward to giving people I meet my real name."

"Can't wait to escape?" He shook his head. "You'll miss all this."

"*All this?*" She waved her hand at the cabin. "Right. I'll succeed, and then, once we're back in Vermont, I expect a big fat check. I hope you've got a successor in mind, because I'm gone. I have a prospective agent already. You ready for that, Grandfather?"

He shrugged. "You loved being a thief. You still love it. Right now, your art is an escape. Are you ready to let it rule your whole life?"

"*I* will rule my own life. That's the point." She finally smiled. "I need to live my life in the open. No more May or Jennifer or Amanda. No more creating great art and putting someone else's name on it. You of all people should know what a hassle it is to live a double life. That's why you never hid being gay."

"Touché." He checked his Patek Phillippe wristwatch, then carefully straightened his shirt over it.

"I want to be an original, not an imposter," she added.

He sniffed. "The best artists must have skills beyond some imaginary fiddle-faddle inspiration. Journeymen would copy the masters to learn, you know. And listen to me, it's a hard life being 'authentic.' I wouldn't be at all surprised if you want your old job back."

A test. That's what this was. He'd been doing that to her all her life. Still, she remained baffled by this job. "Why this ship, why this pipe, Jake? What is really going on that you can't tell me?"

"Something I can't tell you, of course. You'll just have to live with it. You still work for me, if only for a little while longer." He tipped his hat again, opened the door, and stepped into the hallway. "Thanks so much for the directions, miss!"

Damn him for belittling her about her dreams. She'd show him, wouldn't she? To soothe her mind and drop back into May's persona, she organized her small cabin. Decorating was not her forte, but she could see that, despite the small size, it was an efficient use of space, and the whites and blues added a nautical flair, up to the anchors on the bed. May would like the order of it all.

She wondered if Bob had a bigger cabin. How much did surety bond lawyers make?

Just for a lark, she pulled out her phone and did a bit of a search on what surety bonds were. Huh. Coal mines, construction projects, even stadiums and hospitals. Maybe not so dull after all.

~

*B*ob's cabin had a double bed, a desk, and a small bathroom. Wait, that was a "head" on a ship. It was fine for his purposes. He'd worked in worse places. Still, it nagged at him why Sunny, his grandfather, had picked this for the last job.

Bob went over their conversation again, checking his notes to jog his memory. He hated knowing only half a story.

Sunny had come to him last month, all excited about this pipe job. Rob was used—well, more immune—to his grandfather's whimsies, but this one was far-fetched and strange.

"You want *what*? Why?" Rob had asked Sunny.

The old charmer relaxed in his favorite chair, sipping his Irish whiskey, surrounded by all the fine things in his study, not all of which were stolen.

"You heard me. I want the Siren's Song boatswain's pipe. Best estimate is that it dates back to the early 1800s. Skinny, strange little thing, but I, uh, *need* it. Never you mind why, Rob." Sunny waved that question away. "Get your hands on that bos'n pipe. Get it as soon as you can without being discovered, and give it to me."

Oh, it was never good when Sunny focused on something like this. Rob had knocked back his own whiskey instead of savoring it. "What's in it for me if I do that?"

Sunny winced. "I'll give you what you want. What you've been asking for."

That had rendered Rob speechless for a moment. But not much longer.

"I'll want that in writing," he'd told his grandfather, and damned if the old man hadn't pulled out his Mont Blanc and scribbled on his fine stationary:

When Rob Caron succeeds in the job aboard the Heart of the Seas, *then he will be the lead of all future ventures taken on by our family business.*

And then Sunny signed his name and even pulled out the stamp he'd had made with the made-up family crest of a treasure chest.

Rob had reached for the paper. but Sunny tucked the agreement away into the inside breast pocket of his smoking jacket. "Get me that pipe, and you get this."

Rob crossed his arms. "I want a copy. Also signed. Before I start the job."

"You don't trust me?"

Rob had simply stared at Sunny for a few seconds. His grandfather broke and made another copy on the spot.

"But I'm booking us *both* passages, so I'll be on hand to make sure you do it right," Sunny said.

"You don't trust me to do the job?" Rob echoed.

"Let's just say I need you to do it fast and right."

Rob had two weeks to do research before they set sail. He was busy with another project with his tech expert, Frank, but Rob had spent most evenings researching the ship, memorizing the security systems and the names of the crew. For this job, he'd use Frank's untraceable system, of course. It wouldn't be easy. This captain was former military. She ran a tight ship, and she'd hired staff who were of the same mind. Everything was, well, shipshape.

And unlike other shopfronts on the fifth deck, the gallery had a small opening and a bulkhead door of its own.

Best not to waste time. He bet the most security would be in the casino. A good place to note how good the ship's security was.

He stared at his phone, at May's number as he put his hand on the doorknob. He could text her. Ask her to meet him in the casino. Use her for cover and, at the same time, have more of that megawatt smile of hers.

Risky, he supposed. Or maybe it was simply diving deeper into his persona.

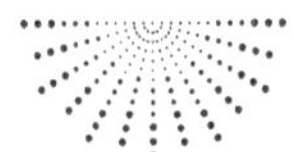

CHAPTER THREE

Jacob settled into the lounge chair on the balcony of his suite, enjoying seeing nothing but sky above. It reminded him of quiet days in Vermont, though those had been few and far between.

He tossed the straw hat onto the end table with a sigh. Miri's distrust of him rankled. It shouldn't. He was doing what was best for her. He always had.

But he missed the little girl who'd once adored him.

"Penny for your thoughts," Sunny said as he stepped onto the balcony, two garishly decorated drink concoctions in his hands. Jacob had never drunk anything fancier than a scotch and water before meeting Sunny.

"My thoughts on certain subjects are priceless," Jacob said, but with a smile, and he took the drink and sipped. Far too much sugar, but it packed a punch underneath.

Quite like Sunny himself.

"You have a high opinion of yourself." His fellow thief stretched out on the lounge chair, managing to project charm with an ease Jacob envied. No wonder the man's marriage had been so successful. Sunny never seemed to be ruffled, never seemed to take offense.

Jacob *almost* trusted him.

"I bet you were thinking of the kids," Sunny said. "Me too. Rob seems settled in. I noticed him walking around the deck, making the acquaintance of some fresh-faced young thing."

"He wants to win, he should keep his mind on business," Jacob snapped.

Sunny snorted. "Women have never been a distraction for Rob. Part of his problem. Boy's too wrapped up in his own mind."

"Is that why you made the bet? If he loses, he might start looking outside himself?"

"Hmm…maybe." Sunny shrugged. Even the man's shrugs are elegant, Jacob decided.

"Besides, you're assuming I believe he might lose. I'm confident he won't." Sunny stretched out his legs.

Jacob couldn't help watching him unfold. Damned attractive man, Sunny was. That thought annoyed him. Never mix business with pleasure, and widower Sunny was not even gay, so far as Jacob knew.

It must be the salt air infecting his brain. "So sure of Rob?" Jacob asked.

"He'll win. He's eager for control of my business already, even if he doesn't know the full stakes of our bet."

Sunny stared at Jacob, all charm gone, with a regard that seemed to want to stare into Jacob's soul. What a horrible flight of fancy. Yes, definitely the salt air had gone to his head, Jacob decided.

"What about you?" Jacob asked. "Are you still willing to meet the terms of our agreement? Include Miriam in your plans?" He tried not to probe too deeply about the reason he so desperately wanted a family member to be part of Sunny's business, but he knew his reasons weren't just about the profit. Sunny made him smile more than anyone else had lately.

Sunny said, "Yes, I'm getting used to the idea of sharing power. It's time." He grinned. "Wait until Rob finds out he's not the only one who'll get to hold those reins."

"He won't like it."

"No, but I built the business, and he'll just have to cope. I worked so much when Phyllis was alive. I gave her everything, I thought, but never enough time. We should have traveled more, done more, I should…" He cleared his throat. "Anyway, it's time. I keep trying harder jobs, and nothing gives me that thrill I want anymore. Your girl wins, fine by me that Rob has to work with her. You sure she's up to dealing with my boy if she wins?"

"She can handle people. She always could." Jacob sighed. "The one wild card is that she wants an art career."

"Why that little ingrate…" Sunny drawled. "Wait, *you're* the ingrate." He frowned at him, an unusual expression on a face designed to smile. "Why did you make our bet knowing your Miriam might not even be in the business when you retire? What the hell, Jake?"

"My name is Jacob." He scowled. "I've taught her to be the best. But she wants to throw it all away on uncertainty in a creative career. Ridiculous." What if Miriam wasn't as good as she thought she was? It would break her heart to fail at art. Jacob could not stand to see Miriam's soul broken that way. Better her be angry with him, better her curse him, than that.

Miriam was damn good at the family business. She enjoyed it. She'd enjoy the challenge of integrating both businesses and dealing with Rob. That should be her life. That was her calling. She'd be happy doing it. He knew it.

"If your girl turns it down, my boy still gets a hand in your business, right?" Sunny asked.

Jacob gave a curt nod. "I am trusting you, Sunny, that your boy is capable, yes." He knew Rob had been running interference for his risk-taking grandfather over the last few years. Yes, Rob was capable.

"Um, not that I'm complaining, but that's a bet seriously weighted in my favor." Sunny tilted his head, a question in his eyes. "What's in it for you, Jake? Why are you backing down?"

"I get to ensure my life's work is in the proper hands."

"You're in good health, and you run things so well, I'm jealous of your organization."

"Obviously, since you're trying to get your sticky fingers into it."

Sunny grinned. "Sure, but why are you pushing your granddaughter up front of the business?"

Jacob stared at the sky again. "It's the only way to prove to Miriam that I trust her." And he was lonely. Tired of carrying the burden. He wondered how Sunny managed to carry his burdens so lightly. That was a trick he needed to learn. Ah, but Sunny had once had someone to help him carry the burden: a wife who loved him. Jacob had never had that kind of support.

Sunny chuckled. "Seems to me sending Miriam on a chase for a pipe when she doesn't know she has a competitor and doesn't know the real stakes is a damned odd way of proving that you trust her."

"You're doing the same!"

Sunny slurped up the rest of his drink. "Yeah, but I'm Two-Shuffle Sunny. Everyone knows I always have a hidden agenda." He shook his head. "All this talk has me restless. C'mon with me, Jake. Casino's open. Blackjack tables await."

Sunny smiled at him. Damned foolish old man, that's what Jacob knew he was, letting himself be charmed by Two-Shuffle Sunny, of all people.

"Fine. Blackjack it is. I need some pocket money anyway. The waitstaff here need to be tipped well." Jacob rose and put his straw hat back on.

"I love that look," Sunny said.

No, Sunny could not be flirting with him, Not really. It was simply his habit. Two-Shuffle Sunny, always.

"Thank you," was all Jacob said.

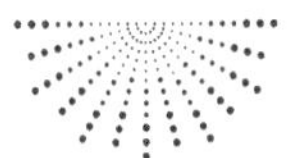

CHAPTER FOUR

Miri put the last shirt in her drawer and double-checked the false bottom on the suitcase, making sure the one item she needed to pull off the job was safe and sound. Good, good. Okay. Organized. Settled. Now it was time to launch May in public while taking a good look around. "May" would go gambling next—that was what an ordinary teacher might be intrigued about on her first cruise.

Something with a safe thrill.

And she wanted to see security in action, get a sense of them, because the easiest way to make the switch wasn't bypassing elaborate security systems. Oh no, it was using flawed humans, especially men who underestimated nice, normal kindergarten teachers.

She wandered the glamorous casino, eyes wide and, to establish her cover, asked the friendly bartender, Boomer, what game would be best for a beginner. When he suggested blackjack, she strolled in that direction.

But, unexpectedly, a jackpot paid off from one of the slot machines in front of her.

Lights blared, sirens went off, and in the middle of it was a befuddled Bob, the surety lawyer, staring at the coins spitting out of his machine. She couldn't help but smile. Bob was having fun for a change, and that was a nice, nice payoff for his first cruise.

Good for him.

Even if he seemed frozen in place. She raised a hand to greet him, but he was staring at something to the left of her shoulder and apparently didn't notice her.

She turned to see what had his attention. Perhaps it was the man who'd caught his gaze, a gentleman who also wore a look of puzzled horror. A moment later, Jacob strolled over to the onlooker and…put a hand on his shoulder. What? Jacob didn't make friends easily.

She almost forgot about Bob's odd expression. Her grandfather and the other man walked off toward the blackjack tables with no second look at Bob

Damn it. Jacob, what is going on?

After he'd just said he couldn't find men on this ship, he'd found one in record time. So much for not playing with civilians. To be fair, *he* wasn't actually on the clock.

Or maybe the other guy was his client, the one who wanted the item, who insisted on being around the job. Hard to tell. Jacob would never give her a straight answer if she asked. *You don't need to know,* he'd say, never ceding control of information.

She turned her attention back to Bob, who'd finally noticed her hovering. He wore a wide smile that looked nearly genuine as he scooped coins into cups, so at odds with his initial expression of horror.

Yes, *horror*. And he'd for sure been staring at *her* grandfather. God help him if it was a third possibility, that Bob was gay or bi and had been attracted to Jacob. Yeah, Bob was no match for Jacob. *Sorry, Bob. Move on.*

Unless…maybe she should start worrying about Bob. Something was just a little off about him. He had been eager to get to know her. Now here he was again, almost at her feet, even though he hadn't texted her. Did surety lawyers go after thieves?

Her heart took a dive. Or did shipboard security officers take on the pretense of being surety lawyers? And wouldn't that be karma biting her on the butt if her final criminal act was dogged by a pseudo cop?

She'd heard that vessel security had improved after cruises got a bad rep for ignoring crimes against passengers. That had to mean more and better officers. Damn, damn, damn, she'd liked Bob. He'd been kind and interesting…okay, and just a little too alert. And then there was his habit of lurking near the most expensive jewelry on the ship.

Bob finally waved awkwardly, almost endearingly, and strolled over to her, holding the two coin-filled cups high. She almost asked him if employees were allowed to gamble, but she'd wait on that until she had more evidence.

"Hey, May! Good timing! I'm just going to put my winnings on my cruise account and then let's celebrate with a drink. I'm thinking maybe you're good luck for me!"

Such a doofy grin. Hard not to like. *Please let him not be a cop.* "Sure," she answered, because now she had to know who and what he was.

Bob looked over his shoulder, just a brief glimpse she wouldn't have noticed if she hadn't been paying close attention. But if he'd been looking for something, he hadn't found it.

As she waited for him to cash in the chips, she examined his butt under those boring chinos. A super-fun pastime because those were some great glutes. Time to pry at the man's cover. Uncovering the truth—and whoops, now, she got an image of him without clothes. Not the point, she reminded herself.

When he turned around, he saw her looking and grinned. "I'll treat you to something silly with an umbrella and fruit. Unless you have a drinks package?"

"Not for alcohol. It's still kind of early yet." That sounded like something May would say. "Let's just get a nice latte."

They went back out onto the deck, her carrying the latte, him with his silly fruit drink, away from the clang and music of the machines. The soft sea air washed over her face. She raised her chin to the sun and forced her shoulders to relax. How long had it been since she had a real vacation? This air smelled so fresh and crisp.

And those dolphins had been amazing. New experiences fed art, and she needed to be fed.

"You're getting into the shipboard spirit," Bob said, sounding a little too hearty. She almost laughed as he twirled the umbrella.

"Mm," she agreed. "But not as much as you."

"Oh? What do you mean?"

A slight pause before he'd spoken, combined with his smile and his so very casual tone, set off another internal alarm.

He tilted his head, watching her as he sipped through the straw.

Yeah, this guy was lying or deceiving her somehow.

She'd been attracted to him before, and damn if the attraction hadn't grown. Sometimes the crazy in her gene pool roared to the front.

She pushed a little. "You're telling me a surety lawyer gambles on the job?"

He laughed, shook his head. "Hey, it was two quarters. My guess is they set up one of those machines to pay off early in the cruise to convince everyone to drop their coins in the rest of the voyage."

"That sounds very logical and attorney-like." She pushed a lot. "What will you do with the money you won?"

He shrugged. "I had them put it all on my account. Guess I won't be paying for any extras this cruise. Might even be enough to spread around for two?"

"Really?" Play it dumb, she thought. Was he flirting badly or was he trying to get her to open up? Fine, she'd flip that around. "But if we're going to spend time together, we should get to know each other a bit."

His puzzled expression was, again, adorkable. "What do you mean?"

"Just that you probably know what a kindergarten teacher's job is like. What's your day-to-day work is like?"

"Oh. I thought you meant...I mean...another way of getting to know each other."

She giggled, innocent May again.

He cleared his throat and took a deep breath. "Anyway, sorry. So, what is my day to day work like? Well…."

His answer fit her brief Google search. In fact, one particular phrase popped up, straight from an online site. "It's all about measuring risk and payoff. A surety is something a business has to do when undertaking a project. Say, let's go back to the cruise ship example. Start with building one. That company would need to bond it with a surety."

"Why?" she asked.

"So if something goes wrong with the project, there's insurance."

"So why not call it insurance?" She added another giggle just to stay in character.

"It's complicated."

He tossed out more jargon and made the whole explanation so boring, it had to be intentional. When they'd walked together on the deck, he'd been funny and sharp. Now he tried to batter down any sense of fun with phrases like "Even those required by law to be bonded frequently misunderstand surety bonds" and "Surety bonds play a major role in countless industries across America."

Countless, huh, she thought as she smiled up at him. That had to come from an online info site. A guy as smart as Bob could make this more interesting. Heck, he'd done it earlier. But maybe he'd used up all his knowledge in one shot.

She tucked the whole phrase into a corner of her mind. Later, she'd find out where he'd lifted it from.

She suspected that Bob, her funny new friend with his surety babble, his chinos and fruity drink, and oh so nice butt was a total fraud. Her heart beat fast with anticipation to discover his game. Because, yeah, Jacob was right. She loved parts of this work. Especially the unpredictable parts.

So. Much. Fun, she thought as she gazed into Bob's earnest hazel eyes.

Bob, if that's your name, you're such a pretty liar.

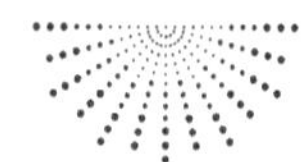

CHAPTER FIVE

Rob wondered if May had decided to nab surety lawyer Bob as a mate, and that was why she was pushing so hard to find out about his job. She stared at him as if he were a tasty steak and she was a hungry, stalking cat.

He had trouble thinking when she looked at him with that much interest. He needed air but didn't want to run into Sunny again. And he needed to blow off some energy too. But he didn't want to blow her off. Stupid, he supposed, but he felt like the air he breathed was sweeter with her in it.

"Shall we go to the top deck?"

"Isn't that the sports deck?" She frowned, concentrating. He wanted to trace the pucker between her brows. "You want to play shuffleboard?" she continued.

"I think that's a must aboard a cruise ship, right?" He grinned.

"Ha! Okay, you're on!"

That won him one of her bubbly grins, so how could he resist? He sipped the last of his drink. Wow, that packed a kick for something so innocent tasting.

As they rode the quiet elevator, she stood close to him, and he swore he could feel her warmth against his side. The scent of her—a standard light perfume—seemed exotic, and he dragged in some long breaths to get more.

He expected her to touch him—she had before. Maybe this time, she'd run a hand over his shoulder, but she just asked him more questions about surety bond law.

He finally waved a hand and said, "Oh, but it's so boring. My life is really dull. I mean back home, in…um, Maryland." Shit. She was throwing him off his game. "All I do is work, eat fast food at my desk, play games on my computer. Boring stuff."

I am not mate material, he tried to signal. Though maybe he was failing because he *wanted* to be mate material for her. So he added, "I'm glad you dragged me away from the casino. I gave myself a limit of two coins on the slots, because the last time I did the slots, I couldn't stop playing. Lost like a thousand dollars. I would have poured my winnings back into the slots if you hadn't shown up."

"Really? It seemed so easy to get you out of there. Interesting."

She didn't seem to believe his confession.

He wasn't entirely lying, he supposed. He was addicted to thrill of the game, but not blackjack or slots. Pitting himself against a good safe, the clock ticking down until a guard walked past, was his idea of fun. But for once, he wished he wasn't on the job. And he wished Sunny wasn't around, because he'd really like to hook up with this woman. But Sunny would never let him hear the end of that, given how much grief Rob had given him about all his extracurricular activities.

No, he wasn't Sunny. That passing thought was dangerous and amateur. No boning civilians, especially not on the job, and certainly not one as interested in him as she seemed to be. He tried to inch away from her and concentrate on topics unrelated to warm, soft bodies.

He pictured Sunny strolling through the casino. That smirk on his grandfather's handsome face. Was Sunny pulling a con on that other older guy? Sunny liked messing with people. A lot. Two-Shuffle Sunny always operated a step away from victory or disaster.

Yes, thinking about Sunny causing problems with his impulses, problems Rob would have to solve, problems he needed to avoid himself, definitely cooled the libido.

The door chimed and opened onto the wide and windy deck. May spread her arms.

He almost ran into her. She'd stopped and was doing her wide-eyed thing again, taking it all in, from the table tennis to the enclosed basketball courts—nope, the ship wasn't going to lose any balls at the height of those nets—to the rock-climbing wall, which had to be at least twenty feet high.

"Whoa," he said and set his empty drink down on a vacant chair.

"Yeah," she agreed, then looked at her feet. "I think these checker-boards on the deck are for shuffleboard, but I'm not sure where the equipment is. Maybe there are set times."

He looked at the basketball court. There were several loose balls in a bin next to it. "We could try hoops? Unless you want rock climbing?"

"Heck to the no on the rock climbing. I don't like heights."

Aw, she said "heck" instead of "hell." Too cute.

"Let's get a ball and get moving, then."

"Sure!" And the sight of her arms held in the air, long hair whipping around her face, was enough to reignite his nuisance desire.

"Have I mentioned I often sub for the PE teacher?" she informed him.

Oh, hell. Now he was too close to her, and she might beat him. Lose/lose.

After a game of horse that *she* won, showcasing excellent aim and motor skills, they went one-on-one. Whoever scored ten baskets first won. Which meant some interesting blocking, sweating limbs brushing against him, and breathy shouts in his ear. She played harder than most men he knew, and they both were sweating and out of breath when they quit.

Her sweaty hair had plastered against the side of her face. She was grinning, even though she'd lost by a couple of baskets.

"Thanks," he said. "I needed that."

He meant every word. Since he couldn't go deeper into any sort of relationship and have sex with anyone that sharp—and apparently focused on him—a good physical encounter of another sort helped.

She went down on one knee, panting, and stared up at him.

His thoughts immediately switched back to the first kind of physical encounter he'd had in mind.

"Thanks. I needed that too. I never realize how active I am during the day. Or how I'd feel restless on board." She grinned. "You didn't patronize me by going easy on me. I appreciate that."

Oh, what beautiful lips. He could find a use for them, and the sweat made that T-shirt stick to her skin.

So much trouble.

He didn't need trouble. He was here to steal the pipe, to get out of trouble, to prevent Sunny's whims from tanking the whole family enterprise. He could not tank that for a kindergarten teacher. No matter how gorgeous she looked when sweaty. No whims. No imitating Sunny.

At least not until he had the pipe. After, though…after had possibilities. He wondered if he could move up his timetable.

"You're welcome," he said out loud. Bob, he thought. Be awkward surety guy Bob. "I, uh, must smell awful. I need to go get a shower now."

And he pushed past her without another word.

"See you later, Bob," she called after him.

He waved halfheartedly. He bet he could have talked her into bed just now.

No, no, no, no.

He showered at his cabin and changed his clothes. Not trusting himself for a bit, he ordered room service and ate, and felt less jittery after that. He pulled out the slip of paper with Sunny's signature on it. Binding, he thought. *Get your head in the game.*

He needed another look at the target and its security. Time for a stroll. Alone, he hoped.

He stopped at the gallery's entrance. Inside, bent over the case containing the diamonds and the cursed bos'n whistle, was a woman.

He couldn't see her face, but he'd already memorized her backside and even the backs of her knees. *May again.*

She'd showered too. Her hair was damp.

He felt himself smiling at the sight of her, but he had a job to do and…

Oh no. Why did he keep running into her?

Not a coincidence. No. Only one way.

Bob felt a flash of irritation and then fear. May was no kindergarten teacher. And all those questions about his "job" and her avid interest? She wasn't after his wedding ring. She was after him.

A cop. She had to be a goddamn cop.

He backed away from the gallery. If she was in there, she couldn't be following him. He'd come back later.

A cop was not a complication he needed. Especially not this cop. Sunny would consider it a challenge. Sunny would want to dance with this cop, maybe seduce her, because it would up the fun of the job. Just now, Rob could see the appeal of that approach.

But it was antics like that which threatened the family business.

I'm not Sunny. He was Rob, and he'd do this right. Dispassionately. Showing Sunny how it should be done.

CHAPTER SIX

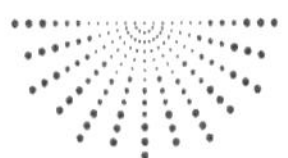

Miri had always thought that playing a sweaty game with a guy was an excellent way to get to know him. Whatever Bob was, he was competitive as hell. Cops generally weren't competitive. Good ones were smart, methodical, almost plodding. That was how they caught the criminal risk-takers.

Bob, though, he liked risk. And he had enough of a sense of humor to disguise himself as an inoffensive surety guy. He was also flat-out fine. Omigod, those shoulders, and those muscles in his back...

Why did she always fall for the dangerous ones? The same reason, she supposed, why being a thief was in her blood. For fun. But the stakes were high on this job, and, despite viewing sex as an excellent recreational activity that generally supplied a whole lot of artistic adrenaline and inspiration, she should be old enough to start thinking with her head and not her damn adrenaline.

A fling with Bob, or whoever he was, was not worth her independence or the millions Jacob owed her.

Or her shot at the life she wanted.

After this cruise, she'd get her thrills creating something new, something brilliant, with her own money. Beholden to no one. She'd get to pick her sex partners without worrying if they wanted to snap her into handcuffs. Well, arrest her, anyway. There could be uses for other kinds of handcuffs. She wondered how kinky Bob could get. After all, he was good at undercover.

But in in her mind, she could almost hear Jacob's careful voice, asking her if the reason she was excited about messing around with Bob was because she wanted to fail, so she wouldn't have to face the fact she might fail once she truly attempted her dream.

That was…possible.

Okay, new plan. She'd nail down the swap right away. Get this done, before she sabotaged herself.

If Bob were legit, a cop or security, maybe she could even find him again after all this was over. She'd be legit then too. She could pass off masquerading as May as the quirk of an eccentric artist. Performance art.

She went up to the gallery for a look again at the pipe, making some mental notes, and oh-so-carefully dropped one of her earrings on the carpet, hidden in a tight corner. That would come in handy later.

She strolled back to her cabin and studied every inch of the layout of the gallery now that she'd seen it enough in person. She ignored the alerts on her cruise ship app about the gorgeous stars overhead. There'd be another chance for another cruise, another time to stare at the stars. *Focus. Work.*

The gallery had electronic alarms. It had a twenty-four seven guard. Two ways to get in: go through the people or go through the equipment. In her experience, people could be cajoled. Equipment was immune to charm. Time was of the essence on this short cruise of only four days.

Time to test the night guard.

She put on makeup, mussed it up a little bit, and spilled a little vodka on her blouse. She also swigged some in her mouth but spit it out. There. She smelled like someone who'd indulged a bit. And no one would find her dangerous, especially if the night guard was male. Men rarely considered women a threat and certainly not women like May.

She ambled back to the gallery area with its stores and services. Damn, all this was still so brightly lit. She'd forgotten the gift shop would be open 24/7 for the convenience of the passengers when they were at sea, and it looked like the spa had late night appointments too.

She wandered the gift shop, noting she wasn't the only "tipsy" person in there. She bought breath mints so as to not draw attention, and then ambled across the deck to the gallery.

The gate was barred. A guard stood at the door.

"It's closed?" she asked with as much incredulity as she could muster.

The guard straightened. His bushy eyebrows twitched. He looked kind. Almost grandfatherly. But old white men were sometimes the worst.

"Yes, ma'am, closed until 10 a.m. tomorrow." He stared past her.

"Oh no! But… I lost an…earring inside there." She wavered and used the wall to hold herself up. *See, I'm drunk and harmless.*

"I see." He tapped his foot. It echoed off the metal floor, nervous now. "You'll have to file a report with the lost-and-found. They open at 9 a.m."

"But I don't want to wait so late. It's a family heirloom and it's not worth much but…it's worth a lot to me." She stared at the floor. "Can't you go in to look and see for me? Please?"

"Against the rules," he snapped but his stance eased. "If you give me your name, I can leave a note for the day guard. He could look for it."

"Oh, could you? Wonderful. My name's May!" She brightened and raised her arms. "Like the month of May, when everything is sunshine!" She deliberately stumbled and fell against him. "What's yours?"

He pushed her away, almost blushing. "My what?"

"Your name. You've helping me. I should remember *that.*"

He cleared his throat. "Jeremy Blozinski, miss. But I can only promise to have someone look."

Tears gathered in her eyes. "I know. But please let the day guard know how much they mean. I can't get losing one out of my mind. I won't sleep knowing I can't find it."

Jeremy exhaled the loud sigh of the long-suffering. "I'm sorry, I can't help more than that, ma'am."

Diligent, May noted. Well-trained. Good for the ship. Bad for her.

Her eyes widened in what she called her anime stare. She threw her arms around him. "You helped a ton. You're awesome."

"Mr. Blozinski?" A woman behind them cleared her throat. "What is going on?"

The tall blonde who confronted them looked polished as the teak on the ship. Her hair, smile, and well-pressed white uniform gleamed in the overhead light.

Jeremy Blozinski flushed again, and haltingly explained May's inquiry. The blonde raised her eyebrows as he finished.

"Miss May, then? I'm Deputy Security Officer Nilssen."

"You're his boss? Oh, please don't yell at him. He was only helping me. I was worried about my earring, you see."

Nilssen's eyes narrowed, all business. "I'm not yelling at him. He's done a good service to you and executed his job well. But I would like to escort you back to your stateroom. I can see it's been a long day for you and I'd hate for you to lose anything on the way back."

This woman was all business, so May stayed with silly drunk and dropped any belligerence. "That would be fabulous." May wrinkled her nose apologetically. "I really am *so* not used to all the fancy drinks. They're so delicious, I have trouble saying no. You and Mr. Blozinski are *so* kind to help me."

"It is our pleasure."

"But still!" Miri slid two twenties from her pocket and tried to press them into Nilssen's hand. It shouldn't be a huge tip. She didn't want to raise suspicions; she just wanted to earn a trace of gratitude.

Nilssen slid her hand away—without the money. "Thank you, but that is entirely unnecessary, Miss May. I'll escort you now."

Damn. Wrong move, somehow.

Miri tried personal chat as they walked along the narrow passageways back to her cabin. Yes, the unbribeable Nilssen liked her work. She volunteered that she'd been with this ship's deck crew for three years, but that was all she had to say. Miri's best attempts at worming out info didn't work. The officer gave away nothing about herself or the ship.

"It must take so many people to make this ship run well for the passengers." Miri figured if she could get the officer to indulge in small talk, some helpful facts about security might slip.

"Yes, we have an excellent captain and crew."

Miri made a mental note not to risk lifting the pipe if Nilssen were in the gallery.

Nilssen insisted on walking her all the way to her cabin door. Miri chattered the entire time, asking questions and getting polite answers, expressing her gratitude that Blozinski would look for the missing earring, but the officer still gave away nothing more than a glued-on smile. What a nuisance that this too-observant woman knew her fake name and real location.

Tomorrow, they'd dock at their first port of call. There might be an opportunity then.

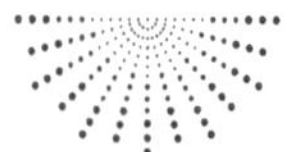

CHAPTER SEVEN

Rob managed to run his program in five minutes—a dry run unconnected to the ship, of course. Block by block, flicker by flicker—didn't want it to look intentional. And then all power off, but only five minutes. Any longer and they'd figure out tampering had taken place.

He ran down his checklist. He had figured out which generator worked on the fifth deck. He'd learned how the locks worked and how to override them in a blackout. His favorite bit of work was understanding how the feed from every camera on board could malfunction even with their independent power sources.

This was not going to be a piece of cake, but he reckoned he could do it. The future in thievery was avoiding electronic devices—he'd argued with Sunny about that often enough. Sunny said he had to learn more about people. But people couldn't be hacked. Electronics could.

He tapped back onto real-time to check his access to other cameras on the ship. Yes, that seemed to be working well too. Might as well test them some more. Why not a look near the intriguing May? He switched to the camera on the corridor where she bedded down.

Bedded. Oh, good God, what was wrong with his brain? He could imagine Sunny's hearty answer of *sea air*. If the ocean breezes made Rob reckless, he couldn't imagine what Sunny could be doing. Probably running a con on that other older guy.

Rob would get that cheerful reckless old fool under his control in —he checked his watch—four days. When this ship returned to Miami. Their first port of call was St. Thomas, tomorrow afternoon. Half the passengers would be off the ship. Maybe he could pretend to be one of them, then double back.

Something flickered on the screen. The camera caught movement. May and another woman walked down the corridor toward her stateroom. He'd seen that face before, and a couple of clicks on his phone brought up her picture. Heidi Nilssen, deputy head of security. She wore a polite smile as May earnestly chatted at her.

Damn. May certainly seemed to know Nilssen well.

Rob got up and walked around his small cabin to stop himself from storming out of the cabin. He'd spent hours explaining to Sunny why he couldn't barge in and steal just anything he wanted. There had to be planning, and there had to be some sort of accountability in the end.

And Rob wanted nothing more than to rush over to May and get the truth out of her. She must be a cop or ship's security. She must suspect him. *Fine.* Two could play at that. He'd get her to trust him with more flirting followed by some light touches, and then some long deep kisses. Yeah, he'd seduce the truth from her…and judging from the hard-on he conjured with the idea, he was the one who'd end up seduced.

May clamping on handcuffs mid-kiss should not be a hot image. He wasn't into bondage, except when it came to her, he was into anything she suggested. Instant lust? Not for a man who needed to focus on the most important job of his life.

He sat back down at the tiny desk. The camera showed Nilssen alone in the corridor now, speaking into a comm unit. Damn the cruise line for being too cheap to install audio on most of the cameras.

Nilssen walked off quickly and purposefully, the way the crew always moved when no passengers were around. He switched cameras to follow her, but within a few seconds, his fingers clicked the mouse and keys back to watch May's door.

It opened, and May's pale face peeked out. A few seconds later, she hurried out of the cabin and down the corridor. She moved as quickly as Nilssen had, but without her businesslike air. This woman screamed mischief, although he could be projecting.

He could take a few minutes off. After all, the computer was ready to go. He'd accessed the schedule and knew that the shop was closed and, even better, unattended when the ship visited a port.

Only one thing left on his to-do list. He made sure he could figure out May's trajectory before he rose to his feet. He cracked his knuckles, picked up his room key, and headed out into the sea-scented night breeze, ready to accidentally run into May the make-believe kindergarten teacher. He set off at a light jog because he could hardly wait to see her in person.

They'd go out on the deck together to look at the stars, although he'd steer them to a well-lit area so he could watch her blue eyes and full mouth for twitches or blinks or hair fiddling that could tell him she lied. He'd ask her questions, lean close to see if he could catch changes in her breathing that might indicate she wasn't telling the truth.

Sunny had insisted he'd learn all the signs of lying, including the practiced ones people pulled to make you think they lied. He wasn't as good at reading people as Sunny—few in the business were—so he looked forward to practicing on May.

That was nearly as exciting to contemplate as the fabulous automatic system failure he'd slaved over. Okay, spending time with May was far more exciting.

He was in trouble. But hey, as long as he didn't live in denial of the attraction, he should keep his head above water.

*M*iri could not sleep. She needed to think through the angles, and that was best done in open spaces. None was more open than staring into the dark of the ocean, the only sound the waves lapping against the ship.

The uptight security officer could be an issue, but Nilssen wouldn't be on duty when the swap happened first thing in the morning. If this was done right, Nilssen would never know a crime had been committed.

May leaned over the railing, staring into the night, seeing the stars overhead for the first time since the trip began. They truly were glorious. She wondered again if she should take a cruise for real. Maybe not here—this was tourist central—but maybe Alaska or even Antarctica before all the glaciers melted. Jacob owed her that much money, she could take time off before diving into her art. So many projects she needed to finish.

She tried picking out the constellations. Okay, Orion. She remembered that but where…her finger rose to trace the image in the night sky. She wondered if steel could become just that color, a contrast to the white stars that she could attach to it…

"Trying to lure them down to you, May?"

Bob. What the hell was he doing here? He must be following her. But how? Oh. Ship's cameras. Damn. She plastered on May's face before she turned to him.

"Oh, wouldn't that be lovely, to lure a star? It'd be just like *The Little Prince.*" She smiled with all the enthusiastic force "May" possessed. "I do a section on astronomy for the kids each year, but I can't say they pay a ton of attention except to ask about where *Star Wars* takes place." She sighed. "They'd think differently if they could see the stars like this."

The guy she knew was Not-Bob stuffed his hands into his khakis. "They don't know what they're missing."

But he was looking at her, not the sky. Oh. He wanted to play it this way, then, seduce the thief and betray her? *I was almost liking you,*

Bob. But two could play that game. She only needed to keep him at bay for a day.

"They're five years old. They don't know much, except they want to do everything right now." She turned her back to Bob. Almost daring him to come closer.

And he did. He leaned on the railing, letting his forearm touch hers. She fought a sigh. This guy, of all people, pushed her buttons. His attempted seduction now—if that's what he was doing—was slow and easy, full of confidence. He wanted to let her make the next move, maybe study what she did next.

Quite the dance they would have for the rest of the cruise.

"I wonder when I lost that craving for everything," he said.

"Have you? Because it seems like you're a man out to experience new things right this second, Bob."

His arm pressed on hers now. It curled her toes. And set other body parts tingling.

"That's true," he admitted. "If I get to, ah, experience what I want."

"What do you want?"

And he turned those gorgeous eyes full force on her. For a second, she was lost, caught by his attention, caught by the culmination of whatever had been building between them since they'd first met. Hell, she'd nearly spontaneously caught fire during the basketball game.

She leaned closer, knowing she should not, knowing this was a stupid idea. But, damn, he looked so inviting, with those broad shoulders and arms ready to enclose her.

She pressed her shoulder into his body and tilted her head up to him, daring him to make the next move.

C'mon, whoever you are, take the plunge. We'll drown together.

His lips touched hers, almost tentatively, but such a soft, sweet caress that her breath came faster. Hell, she nearly swooned.

He wrapped his arm around her waist, pulled her close, then they *seriously* kissed. All Miri could think in the back of her mind was that line from *The Princess Bride* about the most passionate of kisses all being put in the shade by this one.

When they parted, she was breathless. He seemed to have lost his voice.

Seduce her? *Ha. Turnabout is fair play, Bob.*

"Where did *you* come from?" he whispered.

Not a question she wanted to answer. She put her mouth to better use, to brush his lips again. And yes, this kiss tasted as good as the first. She grew bold enough to tilt her head, and, oh yeah, the sweetness and heat zipped into overdrive.

His hands dropped to her hips.

She didn't hear the footsteps—the constant thrum of the ship at sea hid noises—but she heard her fake name spoken in a firm, professional tone, not shouted, but close enough to startle her.

"Ms. Whitman, good evening again. Or should I say good morning. Are you well?"

Damn you, Nilssen. May gently pushed away from the kiss—no reason to startle and hop like a guilty rabbit—but then remembered she should giggle and reel from Bob as if she'd had too much to drink.

"Ohhh, hello, Chief." She swayed. Not much of an act. Bob had her light-headed.

"What a surprise to see you. You said you were ready to retire for the night," Nilssen said firmly. "Have you not had enough excitement this evening? We still have four days left to enjoy."

May winced. "Felt hot in my cabin. The drink started to wear off, and I got a headache. I needed some fresh air." She pointed at the stars again and smiled. "And they're so majestic!"

Bob had been stepping back, and now he stared at her with confusion. He must not be aware she'd been with Nilssen, but they had to be working together, right? So they'd compare notes about her drunkenness. She cleared her throat. "Besides, the weather is perfect."

"I see," Nilssen said.

See what? "Really, I can walk around if I want to."

"Yes, of course, ma'am, just be careful next to the rail." Nilssen showed her standard bland smile. "Will you introduce me to your friend? I take it he needed fresh air too?"

Bob shoved his hands into his pockets, all tentative surety-bond-guy Bob now.

If Bob and Nilssen did know each other, they were good actors. They did an excellent job pretending to be strangers.

"This is Bob, um, well, Bob the surety lawyer. We met at…" She frowned. Wait, if he worked with Nilssen, it wouldn't matter where they'd met. She could tell the truth. "We bumped into each other looking over the shipwrecked items in the gallery. Bob, this is Security Chief Nilssen. She helped me out earlier." Because she suspects something or just found my interest in the locked gallery odd. "When I got lost on this huge ship."

May swayed again, forcing Bob to catch her. May grinned, surprised that the gambit worked. Bob had nice hands. But she already knew that.

"Careful where you put those, Bob," Nilssen said.

May poked Bob in the ribs. "She's the chief onboard nanny, I think."

For the first time, Nilssen's smile was almost genuine. "I shall have to remember that description."

Nilssen held out her hand. Bob had to let go of Miri to shake it, which was nice maneuvering on Nilssen's part.

Weird. It was as if Nilssen was protecting May from Bob. Did the security officer know something she didn't about Bob? Maybe she didn't like working with Bob. Maybe he was a known creep. That would fit his attempt to seduce her.

Except May had been an enthusiastic participant in that. But Nilssen didn't know "May" was really sober.

"Hello, Bob," Nilssen said pleasantly as they shook hands. "I do hope you're having a fine cruise. What did you say your last name was?"

Bob stuffed his hands back in his pockets and mumbled it. Sanders? Something like that.

"Good to meet you, Bob. Glad I saw you both. Sometimes passengers with a little too much to drink do things they didn't anticipate. Or they get too close to the rail. The cruise line had an incident with a passenger going overboard. Not our ship, of course, but it can be dangerous late at night."

Miri was touched. The officer was making it clear to anyone listening that she knew who'd been seen with the boozed-up lady. He'd think twice about taking advantage of May now.

That realization could almost warm the cockles of Miri's heart if she wasn't so annoyed being caught again by this lady who would never forget her after this. But maybe she could use Nilssen's distaste for her coworker somehow.

Assuming Bob was her coworker. They sure seemed odd with each other. Maybe this was something else. Could Jacob have the cops tailing him, thus also tailing her? Feds? Insurance agents?

If so, what was happening here on deck four wasn't just a show put on by the two of them for her benefit, then.

Oh Lord. What had she gotten into?

She had been dumb to succumb to the soft night breezes and the lure of an attractive man in the moonlight. Hell, she was sabotaging herself, as her grandfather predicted. Jacob could not be correct about this—she wouldn't allow it.

Nilssen's interruption had provided a good chance to snap out of it.

Eyes on the prize. Her new life beckoned on the other side.

"Okay, then," she said, still trying for unsteady but not totally plastered. "It is pretty gosh darned late. And umm..."

They both turned and looked at her, with the same politely interested expressions.

"Yeah, we're going to be really busy tomorrow, I hope," she went on. "So much to do when we hit port. So I'm going to say good night. Good night!"

She waved and trotted off in the direction of her cabin. She made the mistake of looking back, and the two of them were watching. Well, shit.

This swap would have to be the smoothest she'd ever done.

But with Nilssen and Bob watching her—people who weren't supposed to notice she existed—Miri felt clammy with nerves.

Why had she kissed Bob?

When could she do that again?

Maybe after she had her new life.

Or maybe making passionate love with him would be an excellent cover. If she made the swap soon, then spent the rest of the cruise with him, he'd never catch her, would he? Never suspect what she'd done.

Tomorrow was gonna be a big day.

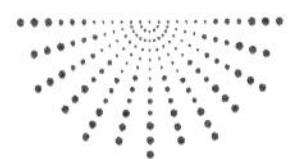

CHAPTER EIGHT

Bob knew May hadn't been drinking, at least not much. The taste and scent of vodka had been too faint on her breath. And yet once Nilssen showed up, she'd put on a show. Why? Not a question he could ask out loud and stay in his persona.

The security chief stood with him at the rail as they watched May disappear out of sight, guarding him from following the "teacher." Rob wished he could ask the officer for her interpretation of May's drunk act, but that would draw more attention to him.

Nilssen had discreetly checked her pad and gave him a smile. "Shall you also retire to your cabin 3024, Mr. Sanders?"

Well, hell, she was threatening him again with *I know where you live.* What the hell was going on here? Had May the cop figured out his angle and the drunken show was some sort of way to point the finger at him? Did she go around kissing all the men she suspected of crimes on board the ship?

Those had been two very serious kisses, at least for him. His body still tingled with their effect.

Nilssen wasn't moving along, so he had to. He made a show of stretching and yawning. "Yeah, as May said. Big days ahead. First port. Lots of sight-seeing." He took a deep breath. "I like her, Chief. Really like her. I will be careful with her, all right? My intentions are, um, honorable?" He stammered that last out, surprised that the statement was true. But at least it sounded like dorky Bob.

"See that you do. Have a nice night, sir."

"Yes, ma'am," he said with as much respect as he could muster.

Nilssen left him alone once they were near his inside stateroom, but he suspected she'd be watching the security cameras to make sure he stayed in his room. She was awfully protective of May or whoever the woman was.

Back in his cabin, Rob flopped down on the bed and picked up his computer. Time to do more research on May Whitman. He'd found a résumé for her teaching experience, but oddly enough, no school in Vermont claimed her as a teacher. He'd taken a picture of her when she wasn't looking. He'd do a face search now.

And…four hours later…

Nothing.

Which was suspicious all by itself, but which told him nothing about her. Fine. He needed more information about her. That meant spending tomorrow sight-seeing together if she agreed. But why wouldn't she?

She'd kissed him back, after all.

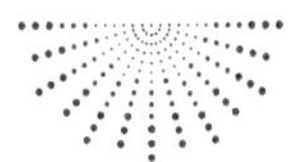

CHAPTER NINE

May pulled out her most flowing shirt, one that covered her specially made bag, the big floral thing. The special shirt also hid the pocket on the underside of the sleeve where she'd stashed the duplicate pipe.

They were due to hit port in an hour, but the announcement had said it would be another hour after that before they could go ashore. Something about docking took time, she suspected, wishing she knew more about ships.

But she knew people, and she'd have to trust that. And her knowledge of people doing things at the last minute told her that the gift shop would be busy before everyone went ashore, as they grabbed sunglasses, sunscreen, and snacks for their day in St. Thomas.

The gallery was right next to it, so there would be some overflow. All she needed was a second of inattention and the thing would be done. And, since the efficient and kinda scary Nilssen wasn't on duty this morning, she should be okay.

She slipped on the practical Tom's loafers that completed May's wardrobe and left the cabin with a smile on her face. Yeah, she had to meet up with Bob afterward for her plan to work but, so far, he'd had zero trouble finding her. He would again, either on the ship or once she stepped ashore.

He liked a challenge. She knew that from the basketball game.

So did she.

She was whistling "These are a few of my favorite things," as she entered the gift shop. The snooty gallery clerk was there, helping some ladies with more money than taste, over some ostentatious diamond waterproof watches.

She headed for the guard and recognized Blozinski. He greeted her with a smile and offered something in his outstretched hand.

"My earring!" She scooped it up and impulsively hugged him.

He blushed. Aww.

"I took a look after you left last night. Even Chief Nilssen helped."

"Did she now?" Had Nilssen wanted to make certain May had told the truth about the earring? Seemed liked she had. "I should thank both of you!"

"You're welcome, miss. Wasn't any trouble. We're happy to make customers happy." He smiled.

"You guys have been awesome on the ship. Chief Nilssen was super sweet to me last night." She glanced over. The clerk was still with the klatch of women. Good. She lowered her voice. "Could you do me one other favor?"

"Well, that depends, miss."

Not a *no.* "Um, well, you see, I've been looking at the Siren of the Sea, the boatswain's pipe—"

"It's pronounced 'bos'n,' ma'am."

"Really? That's interesting! Well..." She lowered her voice, bringing him into the conspiracy. "I just love the legend of how it brings love. I know it's not for sale, but do you think I could touch it, just for a second? Maybe it will bring me luck." She sighed dramatically and gazed at the carpet. "I haven't had much luck with love or men."

Blozinski looked around. All the expensive items were locked up, except for the watches the clerk was showing off.

"All righty. Just a quick touch," he said.

She brightened. Sunshine, she thought. *Be sunshine.* "Oh, I could kiss you, sir."

"I'll save that for my wife." He grinned and pulled out a set of keys. "But for my new favorite passenger, I'll do it."

May slipped her hand into her bag, clasped her fingers around the duplicate wrapped in her other hand. Just the right moment…

Blozinski unlocked the cabinet and drew out the pipe. She noted he was quick to lock the case, which contained items worth well into the tens of thousands, so only the pipe was at risk. Not stupid. Just a nice guy helping poor May, one who maybe hoped for another commendation from his boss.

She wanted this to go right. She wanted no one to ever notice. She wanted to keep Blozinski out of trouble. That was the part she'd always hated most, that her actions might cause people to be blamed, even lose their jobs, over something she did. Another reason to get out of all this, out from under Jacob and his schemes.

Blozinski set the pipe and its velvet display holder on the case. She leaned over it, practically breathing on it.

"I can touch it, yes? Please?"

"Aye, miss, but make it quick."

She said a quick little prayer for her new life, then reached out and touched it. Weirdly, it gave off a spark of electricity. She started, surprised, and decided to just follow that genuine shock through the rest of it.

"Oh!" She let her bag slip off her shoulder and dumped everything on the floor.

Blozinski took his eyes off the pipe to see what she'd dropped.

One-handed, she made the swap, making sure her body leaned over the case to block the cameras.

Two seconds. Maybe just one.

She bet she'd set a personal record.

One pipe out, one pipe in.

It was *done.*

She wanted to dance around. Later. Save the energy for later. Maybe in bed with Bob. She'd gotten the best of him, hadn't she?

Stay in the moment, May!

May flopped down on the floor, aghast at her clumsiness.

"I'm so sorry, that pipe, it shocked me! I didn't know it would do that!" She began gathering up all her things, palming the Siren of the Sea and hiding it from sight.

"You're not the first person who asked to touch it and got a shock. We have a running bet here if it'll do that every time. Never did it for me, but it's done that for a passenger or two." He grinned as he tapped the velvet near the pipe. "Sometimes, I feel like it has a life of its own." He put the fake pipe back into the locked case. "Usually, something nice happens to those who feel the spark."

"Really?" She finished stuffing her sunglasses, sunscreen, breath mints, a couple of tampons, a compact, makeup kit, towel, bathing suit, and other assorted items back into her bag, all on top of the real pipe. "You should sell tickets to it, then." She grinned.

"Ah, let that piece of information get out it and we'd have people wanting to touch it all the time." He tested the lock on the case. "Hopefully, it's lucky for you, miss."

"Oh, I'm so sure it will be!" She reached up and squeezed his shoulder. "Thank you so very much!"

Whistling again, she strolled to the ship's gangplank, and who did she run into but, of course, Bob, looking all spiffy in a polo shirt that seemed melded to his body, and wearing shades that added another level of cool.

Bob was so not a surety lawyer. And he was definitely following her.

She adjusted her floppy hat and grinned at him.

"Hey, Bob! Going ashore?"

"Absolutely. That's why we take the cruise, right? Come with me? I was going to hit this Havensight Mall, then take the shuttle to Magens Bay Beach after. I hear that's one of the ten most beautiful beaches in the world."

"Can't miss one of the world's most beautiful places! Give me ten minutes."

She slipped into her cabin, pulled her suitcase out, pressed the button to open the false bottom, set the pipe—wrapped in the face-cloth—inside, and closed the false bottom. The click as it locked relieved her nerves. It was small enough not to be noticeable, but big enough to hide the pipe.

Someone hunting for it would have to wreck the entire suitcase to open the compartment. And maybe not even find the well-hidden pipe after all that trouble.

That done, she smoothed down her skirt, threw on her floppy hat, added one more layer of sunscreen to her nose, and went back to meet Not-Bob on deck just as the announcement blared that it was clear to go ashore.

They walked arm in arm off the ship, Miri wanting to celebrate. She'd done it, and without sabotaging herself. No more doubts. The future beckoned.

May's bright smile was real today.

CHAPTER TEN

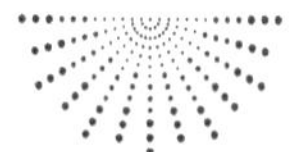

Rob hadn't been at all surprised to see May in the gallery as they docked. She appeared to be super friendly with the security guard.

He still didn't understand who or what she was, but she had to be some sort of undercover security. For all he knew, she wasn't even connected to the ship, but maybe she was freelance. Sunny was on board, and he was a reckless thief. Maybe May wasn't after him but his grandfather.

Another mess he'd have to clean up for Sunny. After he had the pipe. He'd done his tests again last night, shutting down the power without a glitch. Now he could move up the theft to maybe tonight. Kill the power, distract the guard, sneak in, grab the pipe, sneak out.

Either way, best to find out more about May. And the idea of her in a swimsuit wasn't a bad one either. She'd wrapped a skirt around her waist, but the top revealed fair skin, the toned arms he remembered from the basketball game, and enough cleavage that he knew it would be a struggle to remember she was the enemy.

For her part, she was bubblier than ever, pausing to look around every few steps, taking in all the local color after they hit the dock. She whistled as they passed the other two cruise ships.

"This dock is like cruise ship central!" she exclaimed.

"Sure is." He noticed the passengers loading the shuttles to Magens Bay. "That's where we can get to the beach. I think it's something like eight dollars for the ride, five dollars for the beach." A pause. "I can spot you if you don't have cash."

She laughed. "No, I'm good. I watched one of those YouTube videos about dos and don'ts of cruises, so I brought along a decent amount of cash. But I'd love to see some of the shops first!"

She pointed, and they strolled, arm in arm still, over to the Havensight Mall, which appeared to him to exist solely to fleece tourists.

But she oohed and ahhhed over the cheap prices on items on display in the jewelry stores.

"Don't get too excited. It's probably not real," he noted.

"Oh, I know, but they're so pretty! Look at how that necklace combines all the different colors of blue! Cheap stones, but someone put effort into that design." She tapped on the window, pointing to a necklace that indeed had stones in many shades of blue. "I'm gonna buy it. It'll remind me of today."

They stepped into the narrow store. He watched her buy the necklace, glancing around to see if anyone like, say, Nilssen, was following them, but saw only fellow passengers.

When they came back out, she stepped into a ray of sunshine that was only a bit brighter than May herself. She pulled the necklace from the box and let it catch the light. "Look how reflects the sunlight, all those many-faceted blues!"

How could anyone fake being that happy? He couldn't even resist when she asked him to put it on for her.

That meant standing close to her, letting his fingers touch the back of her neck, feeling the silky blonde hair against his knuckles.

"Is there a problem with the clasp?" she asked.

"Nah, it's just me being clumsy." He swallowed down the lust, locked the clasp, and stepped back from her.

"How does it look?" She twirled, her skirt spinning out from her waist.

Hell, he needed a cold shower. Stat. Maybe swimming at the beach would help. Though then, May would be in the water too, all those drops glistening on her skin…

"You look beautiful. But maybe I should be careful what I say. I promised Chief Nilssen I wouldn't take advantage of you."

She sighed and smiled at the same time. "Isn't she just the sweetest?"

If May wanted to charm him, he'd let her, then turn it around to his advantage. Cops, security people, fair game.

He would enjoy himself and one-up her.

"Still, just wanted to make sure Nilssen's not out for me after our kiss last night."

"I let you kiss me. Then I kissed you. I wasn't too drunk to know that. Or remember that. But I'm glad she looks out for the passengers. Not all of them are as good as you are."

He considered asking her if by good she meant decent or honorable, or good at kissing, but he wanted her to direct the flirtation. She must have been reading his mind, because a moment later, she hooked her arm around his "And now I'm on a tropical island with a decent man who's taking me to one of the world's greatest beaches."

"Can't argue with that." He decided not to fight his attraction anymore. Instead, he'd make it work for him.

It took only a few minutes to walk back to the shuttles, and then they were smooshed on the open-air bench seats just like the other tourists. Magens Bay Beach was on the other side of the island, up the hill and back down.

May laughed with joy as they picked up speed going down the mountain.

What was it like to be so full of joy that you couldn't hold it in? Damn, he needed some of that.

They exited the shuttle with the group, paid the entry fee, and looked at the path. He caught her eye, staring at her for what seemed like forever. "Take my hand?" he offered.

She nodded, her oversize hat flopping with the movement, and set her hand in his. Soft hand, firm grip.

They walked together to one of the world's most beautiful beaches, to a scene he'd never expected when he accepted this job. Beautiful things weren't his forte. Planning and order were what kept him and all of them out of jail.

Usually, when a well-planned job was about to go live, he'd be fizzing with quiet excitement. All that planning and he'd reach the climax in a couple of hours—that anticipation was the second-best part of the job. The absolute best was putting his hands on the prize.

But that wasn't where he wanted his hand today. He wanted to keep holding on to May.

By silent consent, they walked to the Coconut Grove, a group of coconut trees planted in rows, though over the years, some other trees had moved in.

May slipped off her sandals and wiggled her toes to feel the sand. Rob watched her dragging her toes through the sand and hardly thought about Sunny's assignment, except to wonder at his own lack of interest—in the job, that was. He'd rather take off his shoes and walk under the trees and maybe get a few good kisses. Maybe swim in that inviting blue-green ocean that seemed too perfect to be real.

Like the woman next to him.

May walked close to him, her shoulder touching his now and then. That couldn't be an accident.

The breeze caught a strand of her blonde hair that brushed his face. The air caressing his bare skin, the warm sand on his feet, and May so close all conspired to make him aware of bodies, especially of hers. Desire flooded him so thoroughly that he tripped on a grain of sand.

She caught him before he landed. "Easy there, Bob." She laughed. She laughed a lot, and easily.

The sun drove them toward the shade. He looked up to make sure no coconuts might drop on them, and then he leaned against a trunk. The cooler air felt delicious. Every sensation today seemed heightened by May's presence.

He licked his lips, tasting salt.

"Is that an invitation?" May reached up and traced his mouth with her forefinger.

The realization that she was so aware of his responses turned him on as much as the scent of her coconut sunscreen mixing with the ocean. Just breathing near her was arousing.

He cleared his throat. "If you want." His voice came out in a croak, and he was real-life Bob the inexperienced boy, not deft Rob who knew how to make love.

That wouldn't do.

Her finger still lay on the corner of his lips, and he gave it a small nip and then a lick, her skin warm and sweet.

Goddamn if she didn't drop the sandals and bags to reach for him and press her small, firm body against him. Holy shit, she felt good... and he was hardly able to form that simple thought because now she was kissing his neck and then his mouth.

Several long kisses later, he discovered he had cupped her bottom with his hands to pull her hard against him. He had to get her closer. He wanted her naked, but not on a public beach, no matter how private the little copse might be.

"How about a quick swim? I'm feeling awfully...hot," she said.

"I..." But he couldn't get the rest of the word out.

She stripped off her skirt and rushed to the water. He stood, transfixed, watching her body spear into the crystalline ocean. She rolled over and waved. "This water is amazing! I've never felt so buoyant!"

Who could resist that? Not him! He stripped off his polo shirt and plunged in. The warm ocean engulfed him, hugged him, and helped keep him afloat, just like she'd said.

He knew his eyes were wide when he glanced over at her, floating a foot or so away. Almost naked.

"I've never felt water like this," he said.

She nudged closer, touched his shoulder, making him glad the water was so buoyant because, yeah, he went weak in the knees for her.

"I've never felt like this, period," she whispered as the water lapped around her neck.

Gah...

He pulled her close, let his feet sink to the bottom, plastered their bodies together, skin-to-skin for the first time, overwhelmed by the sensations, hard, with no way to hide it, and he didn't give a damn.

She licked his ear. "Hello," she whispered.

He kissed her hard, almost demanding, because whatever this was, it was more powerful than he'd ever felt. The water lapped around them, up their necks. Below the surface, his hands slip around her waist. Her hands flattened against his back. Only bits of wet fabric separated them.

"May," he whispered.

"Bob." She drew back, making his name a question.

"I know you don't…I mean, we just met…but…I—"

"Want you," she finished, running a finger down the middle of his chest, stopping at his belly button.

He glanced around. There were people nearby. Not close enough to see much yet but still not far enough away either. "Here?" If she wanted that, he would, of course, he would but—

She laughed and splashed water on him. "Silly. Not here, here. But somewhere."

Hoo boy. "Somewhere with privacy." He slid a hand around her waist again. "I wish we had our own private beach for this."

"Life goals."

She pressed against him, against an erection that so far had resisted the always-to-be-feared shrinkage. He wondered if he should mention that she could overcome shrinkage as a compliment and decided that sounded seriously dumb.

He glanced at the grove of trees. "We could probably try to hide back there?"

"I like beaches. Sand, not so much. Let's try door number three," she said.

He blinked. "You've lost me."

"All evidence to the contrary." She wrapped her hands around his neck. Yes, she was enjoying his lack of shrinkage. "The boat, Bob. A cabin. With a door. For privacy. Also lacking in sand. I mean, I like the water but this—"

"A cabin on the boat. Behind a door. Absolutely!" He lifted her up, able to shape this hands around her bum and strode out of the water, carrying her.

She kissed him as they emerged from the shallows. He heard someone give a wolf whistle. May flipped him the bird. Awfully ballsy for a kindergarten teacher.

Right. She wasn't really a kindergarten teacher. He didn't care.

"Private beach next time," he said. "I promise."

"I like your ideas."

After he set her down on the beach, she gathered up her skirt and wrapped it around her again. Just as he'd imagined, the water beaded over that soft skin, daring him to lick it off. Soon.

She slid her arms into her blouse, covering her breasts, hiding the nipples pushing against the fabric of the swimsuit.

Temporarily.

He pulled his polo shirt back on. It was long enough to cover his erection, which finally seemed to be affected by the water. Damn. Though it would be awkward if he'd had to cover it with his hat on the whole ride back to the boat. He was sure May would inspire him once they were alone.

"I'll hold you to that," she said as she grabbed up her bag.

"Huh? What?"

"The private beach." She shook her head, smiling. "Forgot that promise so soon?"

"You make me crazy, May," he confessed.

She tucked a strand of hair behind her ear. "You know, Bob, I'm starting to think this whole thing is crazy." A pause. "But I like it."

"One shuttle ride coming up. First stop, Crazytown," he said.

That earned him another one of May's brilliant grins. "I'm on board."

The shuttle back was torture. She ended up squished against him, but there was an elderly woman on his right, side-eyeing them. The lady even stared at his crotch once. He took off his hat and set it in his lap.

The lady suddenly found something interesting on her other side. May, noticing, silently sniggered.

The dock, the other cruise ships, the gangplank walk, the corridors to his room, all passed in a blur.

"Your room?" she asked.

"Is that a problem? I've got a double bed. Unless yours is bigger?"

"Uh, I'm pretty sure you've got big covered." She lowered her voice to a whisper. "On so many levels."

So, yes, his room. Bigger bed.

And, a slice of his memory nagged, he'd need to crack open his computer while she slept. After he tired her out.

And he'd make damn sure she was tired out.

And what if she wondered why he wanted to slip out of the room for ten minutes? If she was awake?

Okay... Umm. His plan required the ship's lights to be down. He'd tell her to stay put while he found out was going on. He'd promise to bring back a surprise for her. Probably they'd be hungry and thirsty. He'd need to get food for them.

Yeah, that would be good too. He'd go to the bar—not the one too near the gallery—and establish that he had company, just some hints, not a mention of names. Perfect alibi.

But mostly, he hoped they'd have so damned much fun, she'd need to rest. He really liked the idea of watching her fall asleep next to him.

"Earth to Bob. Have I lost your attention?"

He blinked. They were outside his door. He fumbled for his key. "No, I..." It clicked open, and suddenly, they were on the other side. She shut the door behind them.

"No what Bob?"

She took off her blouse and let it drop to the floor. Or was it deck. Floor. Deck. He was supposed to befuddle her, not the other way around.

"Changed your mind?" she asked.

"Never. You stun me to silence by looking at me like that."

"Not too stunned to move, I hope?" She flung his silly hat off his head, and he came to life, grabbed her hands.

"Just let me look at you for a minute. You are *so* beautiful."

That seemed to disconcert her, because she flushed. But she was beautiful, with water still dripping from her wind-blown hair, the damp suit plastered to her skin, her nipples straining against the bikini top. "I need this picture of you in my mind. Perfect."

Yes, perfect. They'd have wild monkey sex and then some less wild monkey sex and then maybe some gentle sex and...if he could still drag his corpse out of bed, he'd do the job that he'd booked passage for. He had time. Days, in fact. Besides, it was just his future at stake. His control. His risks.

May, or whoever she was, was a risk he had to take.

He released her hands.

"Thank you," she said, and her soft, serious voice seemed even sexier now. She slid her fingers under his polo shirt and pulled it over his head.

Where, of course, it got stuck on his sunglasses. "Oops, let me," he said, and tossed the shades. They landed with a *clink* somewhere.

"Oh my." She breathed onto his skin. "You have a terrific body to look at. And even more fun to touch."

Her hands traced his abs. "Thank you," he choked out.

She shifted around to his back, traced his shoulders, and wrapped her arms around him. Her fingers tapped the front of his swim trucks. His penis, already hard again, jumped as if reaching back for her.

It killed him, but he grabbed her hands and turned so they were face-to-face

"Your turn," he said. "Let me."

She put her back to him so he could undo the top's tie around her neck. She wiggled her butt against his crotch, and he almost came in his trunks. He moaned. "Easy, May." He nipped at her ear. "We have all night."

The top dropped to the floor. He cupped her breasts from behind. She flung her head back with a sigh as his thumbs stroked her nipples. Her mouth opened, a perfect target. He bent his neck and kissed her. His tongue slid against hers, and he knew, whoever she was, he was so lost.

She twisted so they were face-to-face once more. "We've still got some clothes on between us."

He laughed. "First one to get naked gets to come first."

"You're on!"

He got distracted watching her wiggle out of her bottoms and lost the race fumbling with the ties to his trunks.

"Me first," she laughed as he finally stepped out of his trunks.

"You've still got the necklace you bought on." And what an amazing touch to her nakedness.

"That's not clothing," she pointed out.

"Right you are." He lifted her and carried her over to the bed. "Sometimes losing is winning," he said as he spread her out in front of him.

She bit her lip, and, *damn*.

"Let me be the judge of that."

⁓

*H*ours had passed. They lay on their backs side by side, doing nothing more than breathing and perspiring.

"I might need to rest a bit," she confessed.

"Rest as long as you want."

"Hmm…" And she closed her eyes. Her breathing slowed.

He still didn't know who she really was, but he knew he wanted more of *this*. She made love the same way she lived: with abandon, open to new experiences, wanting every last drop of it.

The click and thrum of the air conditioner reminded Rob that he had to get his act in gear. He twisted his head to the side—so much work—to look at his phone.

Time. It was time to move from the bed.

He slowly pushed up on one elbow to look over at May. She lay, eyes closed, taking slow deep breaths. Good. She was asleep, or doing a fine impression of sleep. He might have just had one of the best experiences between the sheets in his life with this woman, but he didn't trust her.

At least, not yet. And not out of bed. In bed, hell, she was an amazingly giving lover.

He gazed down at her gorgeous body, small, slender, but curving in just the right places. The perfect woman, except for some very shady details. But instead of depressing him, the thought of her duplicitousness and secrets inspired him, almost precisely the same way that approaching a new job jazzed him up.

She wasn't a natural blonde. Hell, that was fine. Many blondes weren't. But he wondered if her real hair color was the same auburn as elsewhere. He'd like her with it.

As quietly as he could—without appearing to sneak—he made his way to the head. He'd hidden his computer under the bottom drawer of the vanity.

He sat on the toilet and balanced the computer on his lap. Everything was set, ready for him to hit the switch. He pulled up the program and hesitated. He'd planned for the whole electronic disaster on the ship to go from operational to dark in less than five minutes. He'd start with a nice brown-out effect, then move swiftly to a total loss of power. First, the cameras would flicker, then fail. And then the rest of the electrical systems. He didn't have to worry about losing his connection. He had a link via satellite, with a virtual URL that seemed to originate from Australia. He could keep his eye on things while the ship was down, and no one would be the wiser once they regained the electricals and pulled it back online.

But before all that, he needed to watch the tape from the gallery to make sure there wasn't anything off about the last few hours. Always possible they moved the display elsewhere when they locked up.

He began the feed with the open of business that day and let it zip along at almost double speed.

Wait.

Something seemed to be going on near that center display. There was May, obsessed with those diamonds again. He checked the time stamp. Hell. Just before they'd met to leave the ship. What was she doing? He stared in horrified fascination as the guard, Blozinski, took out the pipe for her.

Oh. Shit.

It took him five rewinds to be sure. When he finally caught the moment of the swap, he slowed down the video to be certain. He rewound and watched again. And again.

And then once more, only this time, at half speed.

"May, what the hell are you up to?" he whispered.

And just to make sure he wasn't wrong, he stopped the feed once more and caught the swap-out at regular speed. Even then, he almost missed it.

She was *good*. He'd been trained by one of the best pros in the business, but he didn't think Sunny could beat her skill at abstraction and pulling a swap.

He wanted to sing. He wanted to dance. The woman he was falling for wasn't a cop or a kindergarten teacher. She was one of the best grab artists he'd seen in his life. Man, when he recruited her—and he would, not even using the threat of revealing her secret—he'd be one lucky asshole.

Plus, joy, he wouldn't have to use any of the fancy rolling blackouts or endanger himself to get the pipe. All he had to do was get it from her. If he could figure out where she'd put it. He checked the time stamp again. This was about fifteen minutes before he'd met her on deck. Likely, she'd put it in her room somewhere.

All he had to do was open the locked door of one person.

A person blissfully asleep in his bed.

Once he calmed himself down and watched that artist in action one more time, he erased that moment of the switch from the ship's records. He doubted any of the security guards, even Nilssen, would see it, but he'd rather not take than chance.

Plus, erasing the evidence meant she owed him one. Might make her think more kindly of him.

But why the hell had she stolen that pipe? How had she gotten such a perfect duplicate? And why was she with him when the job had been done? A way to celebrate? They'd certainly done that, so he was kinda flattered she'd picked him for it.

But why had she picked him? Her reasons had to be related to the pipe. She knew a lot more than he did.

It was time he and May, or whoever she was, had a long talk.

CHAPTER ELEVEN

May woke up to the unfamiliar, which didn't worry her because she was on a cruise ship. But she rolled over and didn't hit the edge of the bed, and the realization dawned that she was still in Bob's bed.

Because the sex had been awesome and exhausting. Because, damn it, she'd liked cuddling him. Her choice. Her new future, all ahead of her. She smiled and gave a silent cheer to no more interfering Jacob.

Her life was her own. This had been a terrific way to celebrate. She wondered what Bob would say if he knew the truth about her. The warm glow of pleasure shrank. If he was a cop, she'd have to ditch him after the cruise. Too dangerous to have him figure out the theft.

She tapped the necklace still around her neck. Bob said to keep it there—it would inspire him.

Whew, it certainly had. She smiled.

But where was he now?

She opened her eyes.

Bob was sitting in the lone chair of the cabin, one of those ugly desk chairs. He was dressed for the day, in loafers, Bermuda shorts, and a grin that could have come from the Cheshire cat. His Hawaiian shirt was open, displaying that broad chest.

"Morning." She yawned. She liked that grin.

"Morning," he agreed and pointed a tray of four extra-large coffee containers. "I wasn't sure what was your type, so I got decaf, black, milk and sugar, and a chai latte."

She held out a hand. "Chai!"

He placed it in her grip, and she took a long swallow, letting the harsh and sweet taste wake up her tongue, and the heat wake up the rest of her. She could not get over those shoulders. Former military? She just might be curious enough to ask him who he was.

"Thank you," she said.

"You're welcome." He looked her up and down, but without a trace of the already familiar playful lust in his eyes. "You know, I'm tempted to put off our talk because you look delicious this morning, but I think we need to get this out of the way first."

She sat up, letting the sheet slide to her waist. "*What* out of the way? The awkward morning after? So far, it seems to be going well. The chai is excellent. As was the night before."

Oh, hell, would "May" say all this? "May" would be more blushing and giggly. Not so smugly satisfied. Oh, well.

He chugged his coffee, set the empty container on the desk, and sighed. "So far, yeah. But look at what's at my feet."

She looked down.

Her suitcase.

The hidden compartment lay open to display…nothing.

The pipe was gone. *Her* pipe!

An involuntary noise, half despair, half anger, escaped her throat. She'd been right all along. He was no bond lawyer. But for some reason, the reality hit hard.

"You rat bastard!" She threw off the covers and leapt off the bed after him. Attacking seemed the way to get answers—and she really wanted to smack him into tomorrow.

"Hey, hey, relax or I won't tell you how to get your pipe back. By the way, what charge did you wire into it? That took me by surprise."

She stopped. Electrical charge? She remembered the moment she'd felt a zap. Was that what he was on about? That was totally irrelevant to the devastating fact that Rat-Bastard Bob had beaten her. "Give me back my pipe, you thief!"

"Only if you take it easy and let me talk. Unless you think you can take me?"

"I thought I did that last night."

He smirked. "Mutual, I'm sure. You ready to listen now?"

Dammit, she'd have to hear him out.

She grabbed a robe from the bathroom door, taking her time tying it, buying a few moments to think. She'd done this to herself. She could have left the ship in St. Thomas, grabbed a private plane to Miami, made good her escape. But no, she'd had to enjoy herself with Bob. Maybe it wasn't just Bob and she'd screwed up on purpose, too scared to face a future on her own terms.

A future that, so close a few seconds ago, had collapsed in front of her.

She ran a hand through her hair. Self-pity wasn't going to fix this mess. And really, she shouldn't indulge until she had time, like when she was sitting in the brig. She might be able to talk him out of arresting her. He might have some warm feelings left over from last night. She straightened her shoulders and turned to face him.

"So, what are you? Cop? Ship's security? Insurance investigator?"

He chuckled, and even in her rage she noticed it was an endearing sound, deep and resonant. He looked, as he'd said to her, good enough to eat.

Except for the part where he'd found her pipe. *Her future.*

"I'm not a cop or anything like that," Bob said. "I come by my knowledge of hidden compartments dishonestly."

She narrowed her eyes. That sounded like… "Wait. Holy shit. You're a thief?"

"I acquire things that belong to others, yes. After all, I acquired the Siren of the Sea." He tilted his head. "Two sirens, counting you."

That had to be the cheesiest line he'd handed her. "I'm not a thing. And that pipe is *mine.*"

"But you sure are a siren, because I'm enchanted."

He kept grinning at her. All her plans for her life were falling to pieces, but he was enchanted. Okay, she could use that. Damn, if only he'd been different. Instead, he was like Jacob, playing her.

"If you acquire things, why are you interested in the pipe? It's only worth about twenty thousand dollars. I'd think you'd be after those diamonds and gold coin necklaces instead."

He paced the small room. "Now, that's an excellent point. I had the same question for you. You're such a great switch artist. You used a duplicate pipe, which had to be harder to replicate than those gemstones, which are worth far more. Why?"

"I asked first." She was a great switch artist?

"But I have the pipe," he said. "Speaking of which, how the heck did you create such a great duplicate? I took a look at the original when I went to get coffee. I couldn't tell the difference at all."

Wow, she really had slept a long time. Had he slipped her a drug the night before?

"I slept through all that?"

Again, a smug grin. "You were tired."

"Apparently tired enough to lose my senses." This had to be some sort of negotiation. "What do you want?"

"Answers. Where did you get the pipe? Who's good enough with metals to make such a great duplicate?"

"Me," she said.

"You?" His eyes narrowed. "Well. That's another thing you're talented at."

That sounded suspiciously like more praise. Bob had praised her lovemaking too, last night. So sexy. She liked praise. She didn't get much of it. Jacob only praised her when he wanted something... *Oh. Shit.*

Different man, same tactic.

Focus, Miri.

"You know, maybe you have the duplicate. Maybe I was putting the original back."

His eyes widened. Then he laughed. "That would serve us both right, huh, that the pipe we want is under lock and key again." He grew serious. "May. C'mon. I'm not upset, I'm not a cop or anything like that, I'm the guy you seemed to enjoy a ton last night. Be straight with me."

"Thieves are straight about things? And if you wanted to be straight, why did you break into my room and steal my pipe first?"

"So you would stay this morning and talk to me."

"Coercive and manipulative, Bob."

He shrugged.

Now that she was fairly certain he wasn't going to bust her, fine, at least the situation could be salvaged. His competitiveness, his fumbling of his supposed identity… That all made sense now.

But he'd played her. Turn it around, she thought, as she'd learned to do with Jacob.

She leaned against the bathroom door, pretending to relax, contemplating this new version of Bob. More animated. More… formidable. But still kinda nerdy in a way. Like his cheesy lines.

And he still had her pipe.

He must have noticed her relaxing, because his smile grew more wicked. "We should be honest with each other, especially since I want more of what we had last night. Don't you?"

She took a deep breath. Game fucking on. "I'm not going to agree to anything until I get the pipe back. My whole future depends on it."

Bob frowned. "So why didn't you take off after St. Thomas? Why spend the night with me?"

"Because I'm an idiot." She sat on the bed, staring at the floor. The best lies were based on truth. "Because you're fucking hot. Because I was celebrating." She glared at him. "And now I understand the sex. All you wanted was the pipe." *That's it. Make him feel like a jerk.* Men tended to fall over their feet to prove they weren't jerks. Even when they were.

"Oh, May, I wanted you before I knew you had the pipe."

Heat rushed to her face. Ridiculous. Irrelevant. "Are you going to give it back?"

"Not yet. Not until we're straight with each other. Something is going on here, but I won't know what until I hear your end."

She took two long, slow breaths and realized he had an excellent point. "Two thieves after the same pipe? Yeah, something *is* going on." This would only work if she spooled out her information carefully. Not only did she suspect a setup, but she suspected *Jacob* of the setup. The manipulation felt too familiar for it to be otherwise.

"I should have ignored you and your island tour, then I'd be clear of all this, and I'd have what I want."

"But then we wouldn't have had last night." That grin promised more fun. God damn, he was so smug, she wanted to smash his face.

"Then we wouldn't have had last night," she agreed. Let him think he had the upper hand.

The tension seemed to flow out of him. He wore that stupid grin again that she'd found so attractive. Oh, no, she was not going to have sex with him again right now. No, no, not when he had her pipe. Although maybe he'd relax after sex. Fair's fair. After all, he'd taken advantage of *her* being relaxed and trusting. She could turn it back on him.

"Okay. Let's recap." He stepped closer to her. "We're both thieves."

She nodded. She believed that part.

Another step closer. "We both want the pipe."

"That seems true, but you have it. I don't."

The next step he took put her within a few feet of him. "I think we might be able to work something out on that, if you'll talk to me."

This time, she narrowed the distance between them and wrapped her arms around his neck. "Do we have to *talk*?"

He hugged her tight. She felt his arousal press again her. Okay, he wasn't faking that. Let him get naked again, surprise him in a vulnerable moment, grab her pipe back. That would serve him right. Turnabout was fair play. She tried to ignore the heavy weight forming in her chest. *Business.*

"Why won't you trust me?" he whispered in her ear. "I could have left you here, taken off, but I want to negotiate."

Trust? Why should I?

Anger flared, despite her best efforts. "Because you didn't trust *me*. You could have explained yourself to me, asked for the pipe, given me a choice, instead of holding it over my head."

He laughed, a deep, honest laugh. "You're a dishonest thief too. I got to watch you in action. Beautiful. And I knew I wanted to have you on my side. Better to have this talk than take off without a word."

"Better for you," she spat out.

He frowned down at her, studying her face for a long moment. What the hell was he confused about? Did he think she was going to remain pliable sweet May after this?

"Better for both of us," he finally said.

Oh, he knew what was best for her, did he? Base the lies on truth. Give him vulnerability, and he'd let his guard down.

"Someone I did trust once, a lot, now uses my feelings for him to get what he wants." That stuck in her throat. Weirdly, she was near tears. *Get it together, Miri. It's not like Jacob using people is a new thing. It's not like I should be surprised that Bob would be the same way. He's probably in it with Jacob too.*

"May, I want to be the exception. No lies, no secrets between us."

"That'll be something new and different for both of us, huh?" She meant to sound sarcastic but it came out sounding sad.

He hugged her tight. She leaned into it. Let him believe it. Let herself believe it, at least in the moment. Here was her chance. "You want us to work together. At least until we've figured out what's going on, right?"

"Exactly!" He sounded relieved. "And after that as well, May. We'll make an excellent team."

She backed away from him. A team? Not so far.

"All right. I have only one condition. If you want to work as a team, give me back the whistle. I promise not to do…the thing I originally planned at last until we've figured what's going on."

He gaped at her and didn't speak.

"No?"

He shook his head.

"So you don't trust me."

"I do, actually. It's odd, but I truly do." He gave her a slow smile.

She held out her hand, palm up.

He shook his head again. "I promise it'll be safe."

She drew in a long breath and took a moment to arrange the words. "All right. Let's say you do trust me and you're not a conniving asshole. We're going to work together to figure this out. So that means you're holding on to the loot because you like being in charge."

"Always." His wink annoyed her almost as much as the realization that he was a far more charming version of Jacob.

"Bob, or whatever your name is—"

"Rob." He grinned. "And skip the dumb thieving jokes about my name."

The hell with him telling her what to do. "Funny, Rob the Robber. But you know I'm competent. You saw my grab. I'm really good." She stopped because even she could hear the unsure note in her voice, but she didn't let her hand drop, though it felt stupid to keep it out there all this time.

"I agree. But you did, ah, misplace the pipe, so it's best if I keep it."

"Yes. Yes, you got the pipe from me. But here's the thing, I'm done with men who think they know what's best and want to be in total control."

"That's not what's going on. Really, it's just that…" For once, he didn't smile, wink, or do some sort of adorable act. He seemed flustered. "I need this." He took a step back.

Message received. She lowered her hand at last. "I do too. But never mind. I had one condition for working with you, and you failed to meet it."

"Don't be silly," he began. "Of course I wouldn't—"

"Enough. I got my answer." She turned away from him and walked to the door. Trying for dignity, she ignored his command to wait. Without a backward look, she left. Next step, find out his connection to Jacob.

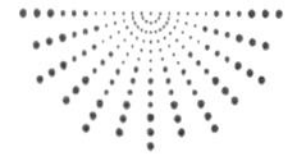

CHAPTER TWELVE

The door slammed at May's final words, leaving Bob open-mouthed, in shock.

Stupid, stupid. Sunny always said he could never read people. But he'd been so certain May would listen to him.

She'd enjoyed last night as much as he had. She'd wrapped her arms around him even after he'd told her he stole the pipe from her and…

Sunny was right. He didn't deserve to run the business if one woman could tie him in knots like this.

She wanted the pipe. Sunny wanted it. Well, shit, of course. Sunny had masterminded this and hired May.

He collapsed, head in his hands. Finally, he swigged the now-cold coffee. The bitter taste laced over his tongue, akin to the bitterness inside.

A little voice whispered that breaking into her suitcase and stealing the pipe to get her to fess up was a dumb move. He should have been earning May's trust instead of intimidating her.

He ignored the voice and paced the room. Screw the pipe and Sunny's involvement and his crappy ultimatum. He had to get May back, and not just to work for him once he won the bet with Sunny.

Should he have given her pipe? That look on her face as she waited for him to comply—either she was the world's best actor, or he'd hurt her.

He opened his laptop and pulled up the ship's cameras again.

He focused obsessively on the hallway of May's cabin for the next hour or so. Finally, she emerged, holding the phone to her ear. Probably reporting to Sunny, crowing about nailing her mark.

The call didn't last long, and a moment later, Security Officer Nilssen appeared at the top of the hallway. May smiled at the officer. Was she calling in the authorities? Dammit, what were they saying? He couldn't even see May's face anymore to read her expression.

Finally, Nilssen grimaced. Great. Just great. Was May trying to get him arrested? But instead of heading to the ship's offices, May and Nilssen took the steps up to the open deck. Rob swapped cameras. Was the security officer part of this too?

May slumped into a deck chair, her shoulders sagging, a frown etched on her face. Planning to get the pipe back, no doubt. But maybe her misery was deeper than that. He had a selfish hopeful thought that she was thinking about losing him as well as the pipe.

Nilssen brought her over one of those elaborate overly-decorated drinks and took a seat next to May.

~

*J*acob called back faster than Miri had expected, just when she was about to have a nice kvetch section with the uptight security officer who didn't seem so uptight off-duty. Not so much a nanny right now as a sympathetic ear.

When Miri pointed at the phone playing Jacob's song, the theme from Jaws, she said, "Gotta answer." Nilssen stood and walked to the rail out of earshot. The woman was great at discretion. Too bad they couldn't be actual friends in the real world, only in the make-believe life of a cruise ship.

"Well. What is it?" Jacob buzzed into her ear.

She wasn't going to say a thing about having gotten the pipe and losing it again. "I have to know why before I finalize it with you," she demanded. "Why this damned pipe?"

"That's not the deal," Jacob grumbled.

"Tell you what, it is *now*. I'm not a puppet, dancing to the tune played by you or your new little friend." She hung up.

She could charter a flight from the next stop at St. Bart's and get off this damned boat. Find a way to steal the money Jacob owed her. Or, hell, just forget it, and use her own meagre savings to start a new life.

Clean break.

But then she'd never have answers about Jacob or Bob and what they'd done. Dammit, Rob/Bob needed to *pay*.

It bothered her that Bob hadn't simply stolen her pipe and turned it in to Jacob. That would have been the smart move if Jacob had hired him to prove his granddaughter couldn't cut it. A move she could have understood.

Instead, Bob had seduced her to get what he wanted. She doubted that was part of Jacob's plan. Perhaps Bob had done a little freestyling.

"You look gloomy. Are you well?" Nilssen was dressed in khaki shorts and a polo shirt, a step down from her uniform, but still reflecting her formal manner.

"Men," Miri said and held up her piña colada.

"Men," Nilssen agreed, and they clinked glasses.

"Go on," Nilssen said. "Do you mean Bob?"

"You were right. Bob, that snake, wasn't really interested in me seriously," Miri said.

"I knew there was something fishy about him," Nilssen agreed. "Should I be…looking into something officially?"

Tempting. But Nilssen would be thorough in her investigation, and that spelled bad news for all of them, not just the rat bastard. Besides, hadn't Miri just made the point to Bob/Rob that she was competent? She'd take care of this herself. "Nah. He didn't do anything criminal. I thought he cared. Turns out he wanted a one-night fling." She sighed dramatically and picked the piece of pineapple from the drink. "Well," she drawled. "At least the sex was excellent. I can't regret that."

Nilssen laughed so unexpectedly that May joined in. That brought a startled glance from the bartender. He must not be used to seeing his security chief laugh.

Nilssen was relaxed for the first time, and it was time to try to get some information from her.

"Thing is, I wonder if he really is traveling alone. I mean, he's not a criminal or anything, of course. But he made some comments… I suppose I should let it go, but if there was another woman…"

"No other woman, I can at least assure you of that. He seems to be friendly with an older gentleman, but otherwise, I've seen him only with you."

Bingo. Older gentleman— it had to be Jacob, that scheming asshole. She tried to smile and sound calm. "I think I know who you mean. The guy with gray hair and a dignified expression. Straw hat? Mr. Mazie, I think his name is?"

"Ah, yes, I know him." Nilssen put down her drink and stretched her arms overhead. "But that's not who I meant. I was speaking of his friend. The other gentleman who's a bit louder and—oh dear, I've had too much to drink if I'm babbling about the passengers. I've got a lot to do and only a few hours off. I enjoyed sitting with you, but…I must go."

She rose to her feet and pulled at her crisp shirt. "You seem less gloomy now? I hope I have helped."

"Oh, you did." All hints of gloom had gone, replaced by outrage. Good. It might be indirect, but there was a path from Jacob to Rob/Bob, and she planned to march right down it and discover the truth. But she did wonder at Nilsson's continued interest in her well-being.

"And I thank you so much for it but…I have a feeling the shoulder-to-lean-on service doesn't always come with the job. Why me?"

Nilssen pulled at her shirt cuffs this time. Nervous? "Let's just say you remind me of someone I used to know."

"That sounds ominous," May replied. Used to know?

"It didn't end well." Nilssen sighed. "She was bright and happy, like you, and didn't always watch out for herself." She shrugged. "My concern there was unwarranted too. Here I am, and she isn't anymore."

"But…" The May part of her, the romantic, couldn't help probing. "If you're both still here…in the world…is there a chance?"

The emotional walls shuttered. Nilssen's face assumed that placid, professional look. "That would take a miracle."

She turned and headed off deck, using a staff door, leaving Miri to contemplate the security chief who was becoming something akin to a friend and yet was also someone who might lose her job if the theft of the Siren's Song pipe was discovered.

Guilt gnawed at Miri. She and Bob-whoever-he-was were playing a game over a stolen pipe, while for Nilssen, it was her job.

Who'd made the better life choices?

Miri finished the drink, but the alcohol failed to bring her any peace of mind, so she lay in the sun, looking at the sky, losing herself in the vastness and wondering if she could ever reproduce that kind of feeling with her sculptures, or if she'd fail like she'd failed with the pipe and, yes, with Bob.

"Um, excuse me?"

Miri started at the sound of Nilssen's voice. She opened her eyes to find the woman looming on the side of the deck chair.

"Sorry, I didn't mean to disturb you again, but there's something you should know." Nilssen held a tablet in her hand. "I need to make a security decision, and to do that, I need your input."

May smiled. "Anything I can do to help, of course!" Had Bob been found out? Was Nilssen playing a con on her?

Nilssen crouched beside the deck chair and showed the image on her tablet. It was Bob, slouching next to May's cabin door.

"Is he asleep?" she blurted.

"That would be my guess," Nilssen said. "He's been there at least an hour. My question is, do you want me to get rid of him, or do you want to talk to him?"

Miri decoded the question. Was Bob a stalker or not? She frowned.

Bob had broken into her cabin once. He could do it again. Instead, he was waiting outside. Did he want to apologize? Did he want to talk about the job again?

Does he miss me?

May straightened her shoulders. "I'm not afraid of him. He's harmless, basically. I just wish…he hadn't said what he said."

Nilssen rose to her impressive full height of six feet. "No need for me to get officially involved, then. Good." A quick smile. "You could wait for him to leave." A pause. "Or you could talk to him."

"I thought we agreed that men are, well, *men*," May said.

"True enough. But there's always a chance for a diamond in the rough, and you'll never know unless you talk to him. So much can be lost through miscommunication, with men and women."

And with that, Nilssen turned away, back to work, the imperturbable security agent once more.

I'm meeting the most interesting people on this damn ship, Miri thought.

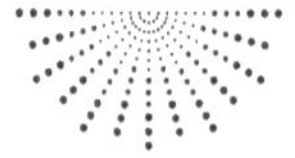

CHAPTER THIRTEEN

Rob closed the lid to his laptop. He had to talk to May but he sure as hell didn't want to approach her when she was with Nilssen. Had she already made some kind of deal with the security chief to get the pipe back?

He slid the pipe into the secret pocket in his shorts and got another shock. Dammit, he was beginning to hate that thing. He started to walk to Sunny's first-class cabin on the upper decks but… no. He needed to talk to May first.

He switched direction, went to her cabin, and lounged against the door, waiting for her to appear. He might not be able to read people but he sure had patience in watching and waiting.

They'd had a long night together and, soon, he fell into sort of an uneasy doze, standing up.

Until a voice sounded in his ear.

"What do you want, scumbag?"

"Huh?" He blinked, alert again, and there was May, looking just as angry as she'd been this morning. Still, she could have walked past him into her cabin. Instead, she'd woken him up.

And she didn't sound surprised so she must have been watching him before saying anything.

Rob rubbed his mouth and tried to regain his scrambled wits. "I, uh, needed to talk to you after this morning. I should explain—"

"No, don't bother trying to invent some lie. I know you're with Jacob. What did he offer you to trip me up?"

He blinked. "*Jacob?*"

"My good-for-nothing grandfather. Don't pretend you haven't seen him. I heard you've been seen with him and his friend."

"I don't know Jacob, but—" And then some pieces began to slide into place. "Is Jacob a well-groomed gentleman, with nerd glasses and a ridiculous straw hat?"

"He's no gentleman." Anger laced the words. "Neither are you."

Ignore the anger. She was listening to him. "But what does Jacob *look* like?"

Her eyes narrowed, and she seemed to search his face. Instead of answering his question, she asked one of her own. "Forget Jacob for a minute. Do you know his friend, the one with a gorgeous head of white hair, charm, and a killer smile?"

"Yes, I know him too damned well!" He nodded. Wait, Sunny knew *her grandfather*, Jacob? What was going on? "How did you figure—"

"The casino," she mumbled. Then louder, "The casino! Nilssen told me about him. Of course." She frowned. "A double con? Does that make sense?"

May pushed Rob aside and unlocked her cabin door. She gave an impatient gesture. "You may as well come in. I won't kill you. Yet."

Yet. Hah. So there was wiggle room here. She wanted to talk to him. He trailed in after her and watched as she stomped around the room.

"I'm gonna kill *him*, though." She punched out at the air, almost comical.

He fought a laugh, way too glad that May had let him in—and that she seemed pissed off at someone else.

But he'd better make sure… "Um, it's him you want to kill? Not me? Are you talking about Sunny?"

She halted and glared at him. "That's the name of Jacob's friend?"

"Yeah. He's *my* grandfather." He hoped that answer wouldn't piss her off more.

"Oh, *really?*" She put her hands on her hips, ready for a fight. "Fine, let's add Sunny to the list too, right along with you and Jacob, since you seem to be peas in a pod, or maybe I'm the pea and you're gardeners, and they're sure good at pruning me."

She lost him with the gardening metaphor, but that sounded so much like May's twisty logic that he smiled. "I'm not with them. I'm with you."

"I don't think so," she said.

This was going to be all right, he thought. After all, they were at least alone again. He could convince her of his good intentions if he could just find the right words.

Wait. What she'd said had taken a moment to sink in because he was watching her instead. Damn distracting woman. "Let me get this straight. You think *your* grandfather and *my* grandfather are up to something together?"

"If that was your Sunny in the casino, then that was my Jacob standing right next to him. Hell, Jacob put a hand on his shoulder. And Jacob also sent me after the pipe."

"Sunny sent *me* after the pipe… How could… I mean… *What?* Mine was with yours in the casino?" He sat on the edge of her bed. "I don't get it."

May tilted her head, studying him. "You sound like fumbling Bob again. I kinda like it. Now think, and think about why they'd do that to us. Assuming you're not working with them."

For the first time in their relationship, he ignored her and instead got stuck in a logic loop as he tried to figure out why Sunny would be with her grandfather. "You're not selling the pipe to a client, are you? You've made some kind of personal arrangement with Jacob. Your grandfather."

"Jacob told me if I got this pipe for him, I could decide my own future," May said. "C'mon. Spit it out. What did yours offer? Money? Again, assuming you're not part of setting me up."

"No! I'm not!" The awful realization dawned on Rob that he'd been had. *Conned.* By two grandfathers. Ouch. But so had May, it seemed. *But why?*

"What's your real name?" he asked.

"Miri," she said. "*My* grandfather, Jacob White, taught me to be a thief."

"Miri," he repeated. "You're one of *those* Whites? And your grandfather put you up to stealing the damned thing. And somehow that's a kind of test for you? Oh, hell, I'm not the only one."

She blinked. "You're *also* doing this for something other than money?"

"Two-Shuffle Sunny pulled a fast one on me. Us," Rob said. Two-Shuffle Sunny and Jacob White, joining forces. Despite his anger, Rob wondered how much trouble they could get into together.

A helluva lot.

"Your grandfather is *Two-Shuffle Sunny?*" Her incredulous question was almost a shout.

"You bet."

"Hah! No, *their* bet!" Her eyes widened, May all over again.

"Yeah." He shook his head. "*Their* bet." Now he thought he really understood, but he had to make sure. "The casino. The guy with the straw hat—he's your grandfather, Jacob White."

"That's what I just said." But she smiled. "Keep up, will ya?"

She was teasing. Oh, damn, she believed him. This was going to be okay. "I kept up pretty good last night," he answered with his own smile.

She snorted. "Eyes on the prize here, bud. We've been *played.* Again, assuming you're not part of the con on me."

"The only prize I want is standing in front of me." Gah, he'd just blurted that out. Not the way he wanted to say how much he cared about her, how much he wanted her.

She raised an eyebrow, assessing him. No, judging him. Aloof, collected. Had he been found wanting?

"Give me a reason to believe that," she finally said, cool as the sea breezes. "For all I really know, you're working for them. I need proof you're on my side."

"Our side."

He thought of the pipe in the secret pocket. He could give it to her. But...what if she were pulling a con on him? He'd already screwed up on this cruise with his personnel assessments.

She stood there, arms crossed. Waiting.

"I have a plan to turn the tables on them," he said. "They don't know that we know. We get them back for screwing with us."

"Revenge." She relaxed her arms. "Now you're talking my language. What about I put the pipe back and give them the duplicate?"

A sneaky way to get him to hand over the pipe to her? Or an honest thought?

"Putting it back would interfere with your great sleight of hand. No." He shook his head. The pipe was all the leverage he had on Sunny. "I'd rather have payback and answers."

Their eyes locked and held. He tried to look innocent or, at least not guilty of what she thought he was guilty of.

"All right," she said slowly. "But I want to make them sweat, whatever we do."

"Sweat? We could work up some of that first ourselves."

She laughed. Not the reaction he'd hoped for. "Hell, Bob or Rob or whoever you are, your cheesy lines are getting predictable."

"I'm solid. Reliable. Unlike Two-Shuffle Sunny." A long pause. *Find words*, he yelled at himself. "And I really did have a grand time last night. That...that wasn't planned." He closed the distance between them. "I could have walked away with the pipe. You'd have never found me."

She raised an eyebrow. "Why didn't you?"

"Because I couldn't get you out of my head or my heart."

She sighed. "Cheesy again." But the step she took closed the distance between them. She put her arms around his waist "I may regret this. Must be the sea air."

"I'm going to use the rest of my life to make sure you don't regret it," he whispered in her ear. "And then a nice private showing and a surprise for them both."

"Excellent plan."

fterward, Miri slipped out of bed and stretched. Naked. Rob watched as she did a few yoga poses, enjoying his attention.

Rob fucking paid attention. In bed and out. A few hours ago, she was cursing him, and now this. Where had her judgment gone? Probably wafted away on the sea air, along with the cries following her second orgasm.

But she'd maintained enough composure to locate the pipe in Rob's secret pocket. Even now, it was still in his shorts, on top of a crumpled heap of clothing near the bed. She could snatch it, easy. *No, let this play out, let's see if he was telling the truth.* She knew where it was and could get it easily. Enough for now.

"We could forget payback and just stay in bed for the rest of the cruise," he said.

She grinned and just stared at him. Could she really have an ally, someone on her side, just like that? *Please let this not be an elaborate con, because I've taken the bait, hook, line, and sinker.*

Not quite. She'd snatch back the sinker if needed. Or just dump the whole lot of them: Bob/Rob, Two-Shuffle Sunny, and Jacob.

"Nah, I want to get to them while they're basically cornered on the ship," she said. "I want to see the looks on their faces."

"And I want Sunny to stop messing with my plans ASAP," he said. "Seems I have things to spend my time on other than fixing up his messes."

That sounded true. Even Jacob had complained that Two-Shuffle Sunny was taking all kinds of risks lately, bringing too much attention to their kind. "Then let's get this party started."

She made her call to Jacob's burner phone. He grumped about her hanging up on him earlier in the day, and she countered by offering to meet him in his suite as soon as possible. They needed to talk, she said. Then she'd give him the pipe.

"That will be satisfactory," he said in a dry voice. "But it must be later in the day."

"Why?"

"I am…busy."

She suspected he was asserting his power as usual, but she let him set the time. "Okay, see you at six," she said. "Better have your checkbook with you. And some wine."

"Why?" he asked.

"Because you're going to need it to wash down the words you're going to have to eat." She hung up.

She told Rob, and he made a call to his own manipulative grandfather. She listened in unashamedly because she still didn't trust either of them. Sunny laughed and sounded entirely calm as he talked to his grandson. Two-Shuffle Sunny, the charming thief. Was Rob like him?

Rob clicked off his phone. "All set."

"Yep. So what do we do for the next few hours?" she asked. "To be honest, I expected them both to jump at this right away."

"It is weird. Well, Sunny said he was going to be playing shuffleboard this afternoon," Rob said. "What am I supposed to think of that?"

Shuffleboard, eh? Was that a euphemism? No wonder Jacob was so insistent about his plans.

Rob went on. "So…I've been thinking of strolling up there with you. What do you think of trying that rock-climbing wall?"

She cocked her head to the side. "You mean the one next to the *shuffleboard* court?"

"Yes. I know you said you're scared of heights but…c'mon, I can't believe you're scared of anything."

I'm scared of a lot of things, mostly failing, and mostly being wrong about you, she thought. Still, there were safety harnesses. And she'd be outside, under that gorgeous blue sky. It might inspire her. And it would keep Rob and the pipe in her sights.

Plus, she'd find out if Sunny meant shuffleboard or something else entirely.

And, if the pair really was playing shuffleboard, they'd be taunting them.

"Excellent," she agreed.

CHAPTER FOURTEEN

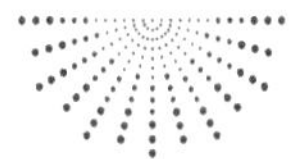

After Rob ran to his room to change clothes, they took the elevator up to the sports deck again, this time hand in hand. Rob spotted Sunny almost immediately, near the table tennis, charming a group of older ladies.

Rob put his arm around Miri. She leaned into him and whispered in his ear, "That's him over there, right?"

He almost stumbled because that breath against his ear reminded him of what she'd done earlier with those lips. And, yet, once out of bed, she'd regarded him with a cool calm again. She still didn't trust him.

He had mishandled taking the pipe from her. But how to fix it?

He took a deep breath. "Yep," he whispered back to her. "That's Sunny."

"His eyes just went big," she said. "Do you think he knows who I am?"

"He doesn't. He told me to lay off messing with civilians when he first saw us together."

"Interesting."

She caught Sunny's gaze and gave him one of May's glorious smiles just before they took the steps to rock climbing.

Rob chortled when they reached the wall and got in line for a lesson. "Sunny always said the best part of a con was making the mark sweat. I see what he means now."

"I've been thinking that we could make this even harder on them," she said.

"How?"

She disengaged from him. "Pay attention to the safety lecture. I don't need you going splat on me now. I'll tell you later." She narrowed her eyes. "You sure that pipe is safe in case he gets any ideas?"

"That answer is yes."

"Got it with you?" She pulled back. "Makes me want to pat you down, Bob."

"That's the idea." But…did that mean she knew where it was? Had she snatched it? But, no, he could feel it there in his pocket. Still, she was making him sweat again, for an entirely different reason.

Damn pipe, he thought again.

She smiled until it was her turn to strap into the harness for rock climbing. Her expression changed to something serious, intense, focused, as the instructor went over it all with her.

Rob had a good view of Miri as she started to climb. Damn, she had nice triceps. And glutes. And she was stronger than he'd thought. Must be all that manipulating metal she did.

Hopefully, he'd catch up to her fast, though.

He climbed, pausing only a second to glance down at the deck and notice the tall gentleman with Sunny gazing up at him. He thought about giving the old guy a wave or maybe the finger. Instead, he hoisted himself up after Miri, letting his hand rest encouragingly on her butt for a moment, making it clear to anyone that the two of them were more than intimate.

～

*M*iri paused about halfway up and let the harness take her weight. After a stomach flop and a few scary seconds, she stared up at the open sky. Endless. Full of possibilities. Like her life?

She glanced at Rob, who was quickly coming up next to her. Nice arm strength, but then maybe he climbed buildings as part of his work. Not her thing, but she could learn to like this. He paused at her side and tapped her butt. She returned the favor.

He went above her, grinning.

"Still competitive, Bob?" she drawled.

"Absolutely, May."

"But now we're on the same team," she said. "Right?"

"Right," he said firmly. And he leaned down so they could fist-bump. Out of the corner of her eye, she caught Jacob watching them. Good. Though part of her was somewhat disappointed he wasn't playing the kind of "shuffleboard" she'd originally guessed.

～

*T*hey dressed in her room. Tonight's plans called for her to look her best, and Miri had packed a dress just in case she needed to wow someone. The deep blue silk, the V-neck of the gown, the bare back that showed off her muscles, and the slit almost to the waist should be enough to make Sunny take notice of her. A freaking beacon of beauty, she decided as she grinned at her image.

Rob whistled. "Wow."

She turned, eyeing him in his tuxedo. "Back at you."

He held out his hand. "You were right. I never should have intimidated you."

Her heart stuttered when she saw he held the pipe out to her. "You're giving this to me? Freely? Why, Rob?"

"Because it's the only way I know to apologize to you. My assurance to you. My leap of faith. Hell, if you walk out, if you're part of Sunny and Jacob's thing, I'm screwed and I'm the idiot. I hope I'm not.

I think I'm not. But, even if you are, I want you to win. And because I still need to apologize for being an ass earlier."

She placed her hand over his palm and, for a second, they held the pipe together. An unexpected zap hit both of them. He snatched his hand back, involuntarily.

She ignored the zap and clutched the pipe against her chest, near her heart. All her instincts said her actions during this whole trip had been insane. And now Rob was giving her a last chance to walk out, to leave all three of them in the dust.

She took a step toward the door. Saw Rob's grimace. But he made no move to stop her. Good enough. She uncurled her hands from the pipe and set it on the pillow instead.

"I won't. I...I trust you," she said, voice shaking.

Apparently, setting the pipe down was all the assurance he needed. He curled her hands around her waist, twirled her around with a laugh, and kissed her.

She collapsed into his arms at last. *Yes, this.* He nuzzled her neck. "Thank you, May." He kissed her, and she drank him in as he slipped his hand over her shoulder, into the bodice of her silk dress, his knuckles brushing against her soft skin. "By the way, my full name is Rob Caron."

"I'd say we need to be formally introduced, but I figure it was Rob and Miri last night and earlier as much as it was May and Bob, so we're past that."

She pressed against him. Certain body parts were only inches away. She almost forgot about Jacob.

"I'll take May *and* Miri anytime." He pulled her over to the still-messy bed. "So, Miri, we got conned. Before we teach the old bastards what's what, how about a clean slate? Tell me all about what prompted you to take on this job. I mean, I get that it was your grandfather, and he promised you a future, but what's the full story?"

She closed her eyes and rested her head against his chest. "Okay."

She took a deep breath and explained about her art, even detailing how she'd made the fake pipe, letting it all out in a rush while he held her, stroked her hair, and kissed that curve where her neck meet her shoulder.

It was as if she was expelling an evil spirit or something. He swallowed hard but listened all the way through.

"I abused your trust once. Never again," he said.

"Actions. That's what matters," she said. "Like my art. I need to try, even if I'm not any good." She raised her head to make eye contact.

"You're already excellent. Remember, I couldn't tell which pipe was which, even after I knew about the switch."

She beamed.

"Oh. That smile is pure May," he said. He ran his hand up and down her arm and had just managed to slide it around to her backside when she broke contact.

She shoved away from him, leaving them at arm's length on the bed. "So?"

"Eh?" He reached for her, but she pushed the hand away.

"Eh? That's all you can say?"

"You rob me of speech."

She actually rolled her eyes at him. "Cheesy line again. I see there's plenty of Bob in Rob." A laugh. "C'mon. I've told you why I've got to give that pipe to Jacob. Now *you* tell me why you need it." She checked her phone. "And make it quick, it's getting close to the time."

"I love the way you can switch from business to personal and back again." He put his hands behind his head. "Satisfied? This way, my hands will behave themselves. To make a long story short, Sunny told me when I hand that pipe over, it'll prove that I deserve a chance to run the business. He put it in writing."

Rob produced the note and poured out his heart in turn, detailing how many risks Sunny had been taking recently, forcing Rob to rush to his rescue.

"I don't get him. He knows better!" He let his frustration show.

"He doesn't know what to do with himself without your grandmother," Miri suggested.

"Huh. Never thought of it that way." He reached out for her again. "You're smart, Ms. Miri May White."

"They wanted us against each other. Bet they didn't count on this." She entwined their hands. They sat side by side on the bed. "Hell, neither did I. Crazy sea air."

"For the rest of my life, I'll be grateful for it."

She arched an eyebrow.

"That smile, I bet, is pure Miri, and it's just as appealing as the May version," he said.

She took a long moment to savor the final leap of faith she'd just made. She wasn't going alone this time, nor was she working for someone else.

He'd voluntarily given her back control, as Jacob never had. She could trust Rob Caron.

He folded the note and slid it back into his jacket. "What will you do with the pipe now?"

"How will I keep it safe, you ask?" She stood, hiked up her skirt, and slipped the pipe into the hidden inside pocket near her waist. "You're not the only one with secret hiding places."

He didn't say anything, and she noticed his eyes had glazed over as he stared at her bare leg. Good. She could have hidden the whistle more discreetly but what fun would that be?

She dropped the skirt and patted her thigh. "Unless our repulsive relations start feeling me up, we should be okay. You've got my grandfather's suite number?"

He nodded.

"I just realized that his suite is probably on a locked deck, and I don't have a key to give you."

Rob laughed. "Not a problem for me."

"I should have known." She took a deep breath. The dress helped, but it was the way Rob stared at her that made her feel truly beautiful. "What will we do if they get difficult?"

He set his hands on her shoulders and kissed her. She held on to him tight and kissed him with all she had.

"We're the best, you and I, Miri. They refuse to do what we want, we'll figure out a way to steal your money. And mine."

"Yeah, but they'd be quite a team working together too. You know,

Sunny might figure it out as I lead him up to Jacob. Maybe they're even sharing a cabin, or Jacob's entertained him there. They seemed pretty cozy."

"Entertained him…" Rob snickered. "That sounds like a euphemism."

The flat look she gave him got the point across.

"Oh. You're saying your grandfather likes guys?"

She nodded, stomach still tight. So much was riding on this. Only her entire future.

"If so, well, we'll sort that too," he said.

"You sound smug."

"Because I have you."

And it was one more crazed, sea-air-induced kiss before they headed out.

They went their separate ways after they stepped out her door, she to the upscale dining lounge, he toward Jacob's suite.

Be careful, Rob.

CHAPTER FIFTEEN

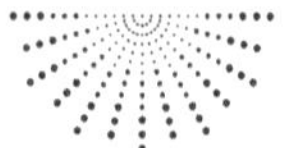

A short elevator ride took Miri to the lounge. Inside was a mix of those dressed like herself, and others in casual shorts and T-shirts. Despite the dim lighting, she spotted Sunny right away in the corner, sipping what she thought was a gin and tonic, watching the door.

Waiting for Rob.

Miri caught the moment Sunny's eyes flashed with recognition of her before he smothered it. She strode over to him, catching his eye again. His relaxed pose vanished, and he sat up straight.

Sunny caught an eyeful of the adorable blonde that Rob had been squiring around as she entered the bar. Hard to blame that boy for her. There was something truly sexy, something intense about her lurking underneath the surface sparkle.

Unexpectedly, she stopped at his table. Could the boy have been indiscreet enough to tell her who he really was?

He cleared his throat. "Excuse me, miss?"

"It's May, sir...I...need your help." She glanced around conspiratorially. "I, uh, Bob sent me. He said you're his grandfather, and he's in a bit of trouble. They're holding him in a suite, and he said not to worry, that you'd sort it all out if you came, and I just don't understand what the problem is. He's such a nice guy, but that Chief Nilssen seems to have it out for him, and I was with him when she came, and I said I'd get you and—"

Dammit, boy. Let yourself get truly distracted, did you?

"Enough, miss," Sunny hissed as he stood. "It figures. Show me, please."

"This way! Hurry," she said, staying one step ahead of him. Interesting, she seemed in distress, but she also was alert enough to glance around and absorb her surroundings.

But she turned to face him once they were in the hallway to the suite elevators. When it wouldn't open, she gaped at him. "Omigod, I never thought when I left that, I'd have trouble getting back up there…"

Now, he truly smelled a rat. But he'd never find out what kind unless he played along.

"Not to worry, miss." He pulled out the keycard to their suite. Oddly, he was less annoyed at whatever game Rob was playing than he was at the loss of an evening alone with Jacob. Just when he was getting the old stick-in-the-mud relaxed enough, to…well…make an open move, since flirting wasn't working.

"Oh, you're wonderful!" The blonde beamed at him.

That was enough charm to light up the whole elevator. "You should go to your room now, though, Miss…May? I'll handle this." How involved was she?

"Oh, no, sir, I'd never dream of abandoning Bob. Ever," she said.

Very involved.

Sunny sighed and mumbled something under his breath about this being a lousy time for someone to stop being logical, but he let her come along all the same. He punched the button for the suite and wondered if Rob was really under arrest.

*J*acob finished his final grooming for the confrontation with Miri. Fair was fair, he thought, as he adjusted the cuff links, then knotted the silk tie. If she'd proven herself, it meant she knew she was good enough. Perhaps at anything.

He heard the suite door open. Sunny was back already from the lounge? No, it must be Miri, picking his lock. But then the intruder whistled, a distinctly male chime.

He threw on his blazer, slipped a penknife in his pocket, and walked to the living room.

The man who'd been with Miri this afternoon stood in front of the windows that offered an unobstructed view of the ocean. Jacob commended the intruder's appreciation of the spectacular view, at least. Sunny had insisted on investing the extra money for it.

Money well spent. If only he knew Sunny also wanted… He shook his head. Never mind. He had an intruder, and he was wool-gathering instead. He was too damned old for a hopeless crush.

"What do you want?" Jacob snapped.

"I'll explain in a bit, but first, I wanted to introduce myself." The boy put out a hand. "I'm Rob Caron."

Oh, hell. "You. You're Sunny's Rob."

"I'm nobody's Rob but Miri's."

The boy stared at him. Jacob stared back, looking for any sign of Sunny in his face. In the dimpled chin, maybe, but otherwise, not much of Sunny's blinding charm had made it into his grandson. This one was more grounded. More intense.

"Buckle up, Jacob, because it's gonna be a bumpy night. I predict sea swells," Rob said.

"I don't know what you're talking about." Jacob glared, staring down at him from the top of the horn-rimmed glasses he'd bought especially for the cruise.

"I admit, you live up to your formidable reputation," Rob said. "Two-Shuffle Sunny is a slippery, hard-to-pin-down seal, but, you, Jacob White, you're a shark, ready to snap at any moment. No wonder Miri wants to get away from you."

More awful realizations began dawning. Tables were being turned. The situation was spinning out of control.

"I don't know what you're talking about."

"I think you know exactly what I'm talking about," Rob said. "And I think you have a damn lot to apologize for to someone you supposedly care about."

"Get out of my suite." Jacob advanced on him. "Now. Otherwise, well, it's been too long since I kicked someone's ass."

But the door opened again at that moment. Sunny, then Miri, appeared.

Sunny rounded on Miri. "What is the meaning of this, May?"

Jacob just gaped at her. What else could he do?

Rob went to Miri and put his arm around her. She was grinning. Almost laughing. Happy. Dammit, Jacob had never seen Miri look so happy.

He stifled his smile. "What do you know?" he growled at them.

"You've been had, boys," Miri said. "Time to pay up."

Sunny shrugged, went to the bar, and poured two gin and tonics. "Anyone else want a drink?"

Miri's smile broadened. "Gentlemen," she cooed. "We have so much to talk about."

～

Sunny knocked back the gin and tonic, pondering. Maybe the situation was not unsalvageable. "Now, Rob, we should be careful about talking onboard the ship. Let's sort this out once we're home, eh?" He smiled.

But even Jacob rolled his eyes at him, almost at the same time Rob did.

"You're aware I know all about security, Sunny, right?" Rob said. "You taught me too well. There are no listening or viewing devices on this side of the door."

"I can explain," Sunny tried. He glanced over at Jacob for help.

Jacob merely shook his head, in disgust or admiration, Sunny couldn't tell.

"Can it," Rob said. "Sit. It's my turn. We're in charge of this meeting, right, Miri?"

Miri had fixed her gaze on her grandfather. "Yes. It's our meeting, Jacob. You and Sunny just listen."

"I see the jig is up," Sunny said. "But, still, may I get you a drink?" He beamed at Miri. Yes, he could see a little bit of Jacob in his granddaughter. Especially that determined set of her mouth.

"Later," she said. "After you listen."

"Speaking of listening, let's get that McGuffin, Miri," Rob said. "Got to fulfill our deals."

"With pleasure," she replied

She reached under the slit in her skirt and, almost too quickly for Sunny to follow, produced the pipe. She made a show of setting it on the coffee table.

"That," Sunny said, "is an excellent sleight of hand."

Jacob snorted. "Should be. I taught her."

"And you have lovely, quick hands too," Sunny answered.

Jacob turned beet red. Oh-ho, finally, the man recognized flirting. About damn time, though this was hardly the time to work through *that*.

Miri actually giggled. Rob cleared his throat, probably to bring them all back on topic. He picked the pipe up to display it. "Satisfied, gentlemen?"

"Not without an explanation," Sunny said. Why give in easily?

"I'm satisfied," said Jacob with some stiffness. "I can see you are more resourceful and bolder than I'd expected, Miriam. I will release half the funds—"

Sunny scowled. The man needed to get over that controlling streak. "Dammit, Jake, treat the girl right!"

Miri gave them both an odd look, but it didn't distract her from the point. "All the money, Grandfather. Every penny. Keep. Your. Word."

A pained look crossed Jacob's face, but he nodded. Yes, that was key, Sunny thought. Make the man give his word. Hmmm.

"You'll make the transfer now," Miri said. She walked to the bedroom and came out with a laptop that she thrust toward her grandfather. "Now."

"You'll feel better once it's done," Sunny offered.

"You think? I hope you can say the same," Jake grumbled.

Jacob heaved a pained sigh and muttered something about ungrateful serpent grandchildren, but even as he signed in to the account, a tiny smile hitched one side of his handsome face. Yes, Sunny thought, you're relieved of a burden, Jake. *Time to live your life, old man. And I've got a plan for that.*

"I hope that means you're not as much of a son of a bitch as you seem," Rob said.

Miri entwined her fingers with Rob's. "I hope so too," she said.

Jake merely nodded, but his shoulders relaxed. By now, Sunny could read him. That meant the man was too overcome to speak without emotion. But, somehow, he was pleased. Had this been his plan all along?

"I guess it's my turn," Sunny drawled. "Yes, I'll allow you won, Rob. Fine, fine. You did a good job even if she showed better expertise and cleverness than you."

Rob laughed. "C'mon, Sunny. You always said that knowing who to use as a partner was as important as having skills. I've erased the evidence, but I wish you could have seen Miri's abstraction."

"Still, you only did half the work. I'll let you plan the next two jobs," Sunny said, mostly to see what reaction it produced. How determined was the boy?

"No more negotiating," Rob said flatly and produced his copy of the signed note.

Sunny made a show of straightening out the creased note on the coffee table. Jacob raised an eyebrow at him, questioning. He'd give a lot to know what was in that closed mind of Jake's.

Still, Sunny signed the paper with a flourish.

"If I find out you're going behind my back, you'll get cut from the action entirely," Rob warned.

Sunny laughed. "Attaboy."

He wondered if anyone else caught Jake's smile at the line. "All right, Rob, turn over the goods, okay? Let me have that pipe."

Rob shifted the pipe in his hand and almost dropped it. "Ouch! Damn electric shock again."

"It's booby trapped?" Jake asked.

"No, at least not by me." Miri walked from her grandfather's side. "The zap comes with the pipe, according to the security guard."

"Huh," Rob said. "Weird. But irrelevant right now."

"It's part of the legend," Sunny said. "Didn't you figure that out, Mr. Know-It-All?"

Rob held up the pipe. "I am indeed Mr. Detail. It'll do great things for me when I'm in charge of the family operation." He smirked at Sunny. "For instance, I know all about these old-fashioned whistles." He held the pipe near his mouth. "I've practiced. They're tough to get a sound out of."

"No!" Sunny and Jacob yelled.

"Wait a sec," Miri said. "Because…."

He didn't give much of a blow on the thing, just three quick tweets, but their stunned expressions made him stop almost at once. "What's wrong with you guys?" Rob asked.

Miri just smiled and shook her head. "Sealed the deal now," she muttered.

"I said he knew his stuff, but he's all about facts." Sunny stood and gently took the pipe from Rob. It was strangely warm. Dare he place any hope in the legend? After all, Jake was right there. "I didn't say he knew anything interesting. The rest of the legend about love, you didn't bother looking into that, did you, genius boy?"

"Love?" Rob tried to sound casual and not look at Miri, but she'd dissolved into giggles. Sunny decided he liked the girl. A great deal.

"The thing I read said it took one long blast," Miri finally said. "But maybe it was three quick, uh, blows, instead."

Rob's face turned beet red this time. Sunny decided he didn't want to know.

"Jacob's right. You are a good partner," Sunny said.

"He said that?" She blushed, looked away, and quickly added, "Anyway, I doubt three anemic tweets will do the trick."

"What are you all talking about?" Rob asked, utterly puzzled by their conversation.

"Yes, let's hear the full story of the pipe," Jake said.

"Let me." Miri cleared her throat, composed again. "Anyone who hears the notes of the siren will become more susceptible to falling in love."

She glanced between him and Jake.

"That is, if they hear it in the vicinity of their one true love. I'm not sure what counts as vicinity."

Jacob, unaccountably, began to laugh too.

"Wait, Miri. You don't actually believe that load of horseshit do you? A horn that makes you horny?" Rob asked.

He'd take all the help he could get, Sunny decided as he stepped closer to Jake.

"You never know," Miri said. "Maybe it's not just the sea air."

The girl was amazing, Sunny decided. She'd caught on faster than either Jake or Rob.

Sunny brushed a fingertip over Jake's face. "So what do you say, old man? Did the pipe work?"

"I, uh, what?" Jake choked out. "What do you mean?"

Sunny threw up his hands. "You fool, you think I needed to go on this cruise to keep an eye on Rob? He does fine on his own. Hell, they'd have done fine without us. We're here because I wanted *you* here. With me."

Jake stiffened. "You're not gay," he snapped. "You were married. To a woman!"

"A wonderful woman who I'll never forget. But it's time to move on," Sunny said as grief and loved closed his throat. Phyllis would have liked Jake.

"Did Grandma know about this?" Rob choked out.

"Oh, jeez, boy, don't you know that sexuality is a spectrum? I thought your generation was smarter than that. And I never kept secrets from my Phyllis." He spoke to Rob but kept his eyes on Jake. "Get up to speed. I can love your grandmother and also, well... How about it, Jake?"

"Oh my God," Miri whispered. Sunny ignored that too, because Jake was still frozen. Shock? Anger? Lust, hopefully?

"You..." Jake narrowed his eyes. "Two-Shuffle Sunny. You said it was about the bet, but you've been trying to *seduce* me this whole cruise."

Jake almost sounded indignant. Probably didn't like the loss of control.

"Signal the trumpets and the brass band, everyone. Jacob White's finally caught a clue." Sunny reached out his hand to the other man, praying it wasn't shaking. He'd never thought he'd find someone as suited for him as Phyllis. But sometimes life threw you a life preserver. "You finally got it, old fool."

Jacob smiled, enclosed the outstretched hand, brought it to his mouth, and kissed it, a lingering touch of lips to skin.

Ah, lust, I've missed you, Sunny thought.

"Yes, I think I finally do get it," Jake said.

Sunny could do nothing but grin like the old fool for love that he was.

"Let's go," he heard Miri saying. "We're in the way here, Rob."

"But...but..." Rob sputtered.

"Forget it, Rob. It's the pipe. And the sea air." She laughed. "My cabin or yours?"

Jake closed on him, and Sunny never heard the kids shut the door as they left.

EPILOGUE

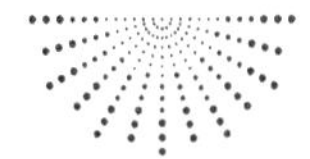

S*ix months later.*

The flower arrangements were lush, the music divine, and the weather perfect.

Miri stood in the shade near the garden that had been filled with white tents and fairy lights. Her fitted silk dress was a shade of peach she didn't think suited her but Jacob had told her made her almost as lovely as a diamond. For a moment, she thought he was joking, but no, he'd given her a compliment.

After he'd said that, she had to buy the dress.

Jacob had mellowed considerably and grown better and better at showing signs of approval. She knew it was the effect of one person whose name fit him perfectly: the jolly and relentless Sunny.

"Hey, you seen Rob?" a guy with a voice like a buzz saw asked another man. She thought it might have been Fishsticks talking to someone else named Pikken. She hadn't learned the names of the Caron gang yet. But she had managed to stay out of their business, no matter how much Rob coaxed her to join the combined gang and try for some extractions from unsavory characters with too much money.

At least he gave up easily when she said no. And she encouraged him to keep trying, because as she put it, she loved the incentives he offered. He usually began with enticing kisses and worked his way over her body to do incredible things with that coaxing mouth.

"It's supposed to start any second," the guy said again. But there was still no sign of Rob.

Panic filled her. Was he going to be late to the wedding? Rob was never late to important events. What was going on?

Sunny appeared at her side. "You ready?" he whispered. He touched her cheek. His hand was freezing cold, and she thought it trembled, so she seized it.

"This is a really, ah, interesting, way of doing things," she murmured.

"But it's one hundred percent perfect, I promise you," Sunny said. He craned his neck, trying to see around the people standing in the garden. His shoulders relaxed. "Oh good. The boys are finally here."

His relief told her that the event itself hadn't made him nervous and turned his hands into ice cubes. Sunny had been worried the main characters wouldn't show up.

The crowd drifted to the chairs, and yes, indeed, there stood Rob and Jacob, her grandfather, both before the altar, which was actually some kind of sundial that Jacob had stolen from a European garden.

The music grew louder. Not the wedding march, thank goodness, but some kind of sea shanty. It seemed appropriate, as Rob pointed out.

She and Sunny ambled along the path. There'd been no rehearsal, but she kept pace with him easily.

"Thank you," she whispered to him as they drew near.

"For what?"

"For doing this with me today. For Rob. For everything. Just answer me one question, really this time. No more kidding around about friendly rivalries. What made you make that stupid bet with Jacob in the first place?"

"I found he was the one person who understood me since my late wife. I wanted to spend time with him. That bet kept us together. Worked well, don't you think?"

"It was almost disaster," she noted.

"Almost, but that's the fun of it," drawled Two-Shuffle Sunny.

Ah. She knew all about the thrill of working together.

They'd reached the altar. In a tux, Jacob looked distinguished as usual, though the added warmth in his eyes that she had never seen before made him positively handsome.

Someone else took her hand.

Rob.

She squeezed his fingers once, then let go. They hadn't asked anyone to save them chairs—another problem with no rehearsals. That meant she and Rob had to move to the side of the canopy so no one's view was blocked.

As she stood, wishing she'd worn flat shoes, Rob took her hand again. This time, he slipped a little silver object to her that sizzled her palm. He leaned so close, she could feel his warm breath brush her ear as he whispered, "When this is over, I'm going to blow this thing. One long whistle. What do you think?"

She shook her head but had trouble hiding her grin as she watched their grandfathers get married.

*R*ob grinned too. He was still mildly surprised. Sunny getting it on with a guy? Not a problem for Rob, past the extreme ick factor of sexxing grandparents. But now he realized that Sunny's dangerous jobs had been a way of dealing with his grief. A grief he'd always bear, Rob thought, but now he could have happiness too. Jacob steadied him.

Thinking of steadying influences, Rob knew he had gained someone who could do the opposite for him and put a spring in his step. He put his arm around Miri, who looked like spring. May, really.

May. Spring. New beginnings.

And he loved every glittering facet, surface or deep, of his happy ex-thief.

The package arrived on board the *Heart of the Sea* addressed to "Security Chief Nilssen." No return address on the plain box, though there was a small "From May" written in pink on one side.

No need to send it through the X-ray machine, then. Nilssen smiled as she thought of the bright blonde from the cruise almost eight months ago now. After that one dustup with Bob, they'd seemed quite happy together, and their reflected joy had warmed Nilssen's heart.

At least someone had done the right thing by the one they loved.

Inside the package was a white box. She slipped the cover off to reveal a silver boatswain's pipe that looked to be a duplicate of the Siren's Song.

Hands shaking, Nilssen read the note:

This lived up to the legend and brought all of us love. It felt churlish to keep it and not spread that love around. Use it in good health.

May & Bob

P.S. The one in the display case is a duplicate. Might want to switch them back.

.

ABOUT THE AUTHORS

Corrina Lawson is a writer, mom, geek and sometime superhero. She is a former newspaper reporter with a degree in journalism from Boston University. Corrina is currently Content Director of Geek Mom and a core contributor to its brother site, Geek Dad.

Sign up for her newsletter at https://corrina-lawson.com/ for fun stuff like events at comic cons, conferences, and my favorite geeky reads.

Summer Devon is the alter ego of Kate Rothwell. Kate/Summer lives in Connecticut, USA, and also writes books, usually gaslight historicals, as Kate. Nearly all of her stories are m/m romance so this is a change of pace.

For more information about Summer and Kate, go to http://katerothwell.com or http://summerdevon.com. Summer can also be found at https://www.facebook.com/S.DevonAuthor

The Hanged Man's Hero
Hot Under the Collar

Seducing Stephen
    The Gentleman and the Rogue
    The Nobleman and the Spy
    Sin and the Preacher's Son
    The Psychic and the Sleuth
    The Gentleman's Keeper
    The Gentleman's Madness
    Mending Him
    The Bohemian and the Banker

Victorian Holiday Hearts series:
    Simon and the Christmas Spirit
    Will and the Valentine Saint
    Mike and the Spring Awakening
    Delaney and the Autumn Masque

TITLES WRITTEN AS KATE ROTHWELL

Titles Written as Kate Rothwell (m/f romance)

Somebody Wonderful
    Somebody to Love
    Someone to Cherish
    Thank You, Mrs. M
    Seducing Miss Dunaway (free novella)
    Protecting Miss Samuels
    Powder of Sin
    Her Mad Baron
    Love Between the Lines
    Mademoiselle Makes a Match
    The Earl, a Girl, and a Promise